DEADLY MAGIC DANCE

P A WILSON

FREE EBOOK

Claim your copy of Spells and Other Charms when you use the QR code to sign up for my newsletter and learn more about Quinn and Cate's past.

CHAPTER ONE

Agnes locked her car and then unlocked it again. She took her phone, a notepad and pencil from her purse before tucking it under the passenger seat. Dropping her keys and supplies in her pocket, she walked away to join the four people standing outside the abandoned machine shop. Should she disclose the charm sitting on the dashboard? So many people had them, and they really only worked the same way as a car alarm. No. It had no bearing on her ability to complete the job.

The majority of buildings in the area were abandoned. A good place to commit crimes. It wouldn't be long before developers converted the old buildings to condos or tore them down to build towers. The air smelled of rust and over-grown greenery, but behind those scents lurked a coppery burn and something rotting.

Her first day on the job and she was already nervous about being at a crime scene. Assessing magic for use in police work wasn't so much of an issue. She thought of it as a tool, not a weapon as so many of the other defense lawyers did.

She'd met Mamoru Yamana at HOP-D, but the others

were complete strangers. She guessed at what they were as she crossed the road. The easiest was the fairy: wings, usually no bigger than a two-year-old, and unable to settle. The woman, perhaps a sprite: tall, spiky green hair like grass, and her skin textured like a tree trunk. The male, maybe in his twenties by the look of him, could be anything. Red-haired and pale-skinned like the sidhe, but so nervous she couldn't believe he was part of that glamorous and confident community.

"Agnes," Mamoru said as she approached, "let me introduce you before we go in."

He named the people: The sprite, Fernlight, the fairy, Bramble, King Bramble apparently, the other a wizard, Lionel. "You'll meet the rest of the team when you return to the office."

"I'm Agnes Swiftwing," she said. "I hope to get to know you better, but perhaps we should start on the case."

"You are going to follow us around, right?" Bramble asked. "How can we be sure you won't get in the way? We only work very important cases."

"I am here to observe and assess. I promise I won't be a distraction."

She noticed Mamoru kept quiet, perhaps giving her the chance to build her own relationship. Although, he looked odd, maybe ill.

"It's just good to be on my first case," Lionel said. "I hope I get it right. I wouldn't want a spell to go wrong when you are around."

"Do spells go wrong often?" That was something she hadn't anticipated. It would affect the assessment.

The sprite chuckled and touched Lionel's arm. "No. Lionel is nervous. Perhaps we should go in now, Mamoru."

"In a moment," he said. "I want you to be prepared for what is inside the building. It is a... difficult scene."

"Perhaps you should wait outside," Bramble said to Agnes, "at least until we learn if magic will help."

The fairy seemed genuinely concerned. She had to remind herself that magical folk were not like humans. They could be charming and polite, but no one knew if that covered a psychologically twisted personality, at least from a human perspective. *Don't automatically like them. Be professional.*

"What does it look like?" she asked. Better to be prepared than to faint on her first crime scene.

"I prefer to let you see that for yourselves," Mamoru said. "Your first reactions are important."

"Then how will we know if we can handle it?" Lionel asked. His Adam's apple bounced as he swallowed.

"You don't trust us?" Fernlight asked. "You want to learn if we recognize the crime? You think the criminal is magical?"

He's surprised. Agnes thought this a cohesive team, but there was suspicion on both sides. This assignment was going to be interesting.

"I do trust you," Mamoru said. "You will understand why I am cautious when we go in."

"Fine," Bramble said. "I am sure I will be able to handle it. I think Fernlight and Lionel have seen many nasty things, so you should only worry about the human."

Agnes bit her lips to hide the smile. Bramble was not a child, no matter how much he reminded her of one. "If I think I will have trouble, I'll leave before I embarrass anyone."

Mamoru seemed to be considering their answers.

How bad is this crime?

"When we go inside, you will be required to wear protective covering. We do not want the scene to be compromised by your DNA. There are two constables on site. Please let me do the talking. We are the official authority, but the local police do not care much for HOP-D."

"Because they don't like magical folk?" Bramble asked.

"Because they are suspicious of anyone who isn't a cop," Agnes said. "Believe me, most of the police are good people, but some have a long history of dealing badly with my ancestors and still, some of my relatives."

"You are one of the first people," Fernlight said. "Don't your spirits protect you?"

Agnes chuckled. "They are more interested in the bigger questions in life. The daily activities of humans don't seem to register on their consciences."

"If you are ready," Mamoru said, "follow me."

CHAPTER TWO

Bramble flitted to the door leading to their crime scene. Now they would get a start on the case.

"Hold on," a policeman said. "You can't just go in there."

Bramble flew back to Mamoru. Perhaps the human had not noticed HOP-D was in charge. He looked at Mamoru. He should wear a uniform or a big badge so this didn't happen in the future.

Mamoru took a step forward. "This is our crime scene for the moment," he said, holding out a card.

The policeman looked at the card and then at Mamoru. "I didn't get any orders about that."

"Your sergeant should have communicated by now." He put the card away. "No matter. You don't need orders to move aside for HOP-D."

The policeman looked at the rest of the group. Bramble could see he was going to say no.

"Only the humans," he said after a moment. "I didn't receive anything saying random fairy folk can wander in for a look at the body."

"I am the only fairy," Bramble said, floating forward. "We are not random. We are consultants for HOP-D."

"You're all fairies to me, buddy." The policeman stepped to block the doorway. "If you work for HOP-D, they can clear you."

Bramble looked at Fernlight. How was she reacting to the obstruction? She just watched, as did Lionel and Agnes. Didn't they understand this was wrong? This policeman was not paying attention to Mamoru. He was going to stop them from finding out what happened. He spun in the air to tell Mamoru to fix it.

"One moment," Mamoru said before Bramble had a chance to speak. He pulled out his phone and pressed one button. He spoke quietly and then handed the phone to the policeman. "Your chief constable."

The policeman looked surprised. He held the phone to his ear, which was disappointing because Bramble wouldn't be able to hear what the other person said.

"Yes, sir. I understand. Yes, sir." He handed the phone back to Mamoru. "You'll need protective gear. It's in a box outside the crime scene. No exceptions. If the gear doesn't fit, you don't go in."

"Thank you," Mamoru said. He looked at Bramble. "There may not be a suit small enough for you. And it likely won't have openings for wings."

That was not going to keep him outside the room. "My wings will be fine inside a suit; I will make room. I can grow, and maybe Lionel can shrink the suit to fit. Although, I can create a spell to keep me from leaving little bits of myself in the room. I can do that for everyone."

"You can tell me about the spell for the future," Agnes said. "For now, you need to wear whatever is provided. Although I think you'll make a lot of friends if you can come up with a substitute for the crinkly, sweaty outfits we need to wear."

Maybe she would be a good team member, Bramble thought. He followed Mamoru into the short hall. He smelled something very bad ahead of them.

Everyone except Lionel put on a white suit, and bags to cover their shoes. Then gloves. Bramble grew as big as he could and climbed into the smallest suit in the box. It was still three times too big for him. Lionel looked him over and took some metal clips from his pocket. "No need for a spell," he said. "We can bunch it up enough to work. And you can tie knots in the shoe bags."

When the suit was clipped it worked okay, but flying was going to be uncomfortable. Bramble sorted through the gloves and found some small enough to work. They waited for Lionel to be ready and then Mamoru looked into the room filled with the stink of rotten meat.

"Before we go in," Mamoru said, turning back to them, "I need to know you are still prepared for what you will encounter."

Lionel almost shouted at him to get on with it. What stopped him was the same thing that made him frustrated. Mamoru knew them. Maybe not Agnes, but he was aware of what Fernlight and Bramble had already seen in previous cases. How bad could this be? "I might have a solution," he said. "Calming charms." He dug into his pocket for the lemon candies he'd used to store the magic.

"I will be fine," Bramble said, "and so will Fernlight. We saw the place where the bodies were left by the Birgit woman."

"I don't need it for me," Lionel said. "I can deal with whatever it is." He wasn't sure that was true but promised himself if he felt faint or sick, he would leave the room. "Agnes?"

She looked at the candy, and Lionel reached closer so she could take one. "It will taste exactly like lemon."

"No, thank you. I think I should keep a clear mind. I am not unprotected." She fingered the pendant hanging on a silver chain around her neck. "If I am to analyze your use of magic, I should not be under its influence."

Not their magic, she meant. Her pendant was an amulet, but the magic was old and passive.

"Do you need one?" he asked Mamoru. "Perhaps you haven't seen what's through the door."

"I have seen it. It will not be better because of that, but I am somewhat used to the horrors we inflict on others."

Bramble started flying back and forth. "We cannot stand around all day. Mamoru, thank you for your concern, but we must see the crime now, before more police come and try to stop us."

Mamoru gave a tiny nod and checked his gloves were snug. "None of the police will stop us, Bramble. But the crime scene team needs to get in soon. Follow me."

CHAPTER THREE

Agnes kept her eyes on the floor as they entered the room. She recognized the smell of decomposition, heavy and ripe. This time the odor carried a sharp tang she didn't recognize. And she heard creaking and bumping sounds that didn't match with a dead body.

No one else reacted so she looked; a dead human hung from a rope wrapped around a beam. The body was emaciated, damaged by cuts and bruises — and blue. That was not the oddest thing about it. The creak and bump, it turned out, were coming from the rope as the corpse danced. Not a swaying in the wind, but a jerking dance that bounced the rope on the beam.

She'd seen her share of dead drug users. Sad, but pretty common. Overdoses were so easy with the powerful opioids circulating these days. This was nothing like that.

She looked around. None of the magical folk were talking, just looking at the body. Perhaps they thought this was normal.

The tang was stronger now.

"Do we know why that is happening?" she asked Mamoru.

"No. I am hoping our colleagues will have answers." He stepped back to allow Fernlight and Lionel to get closer. Bramble was already floating around, out of reach of the moving arms and legs.

"It's magic," Bramble said, "but nothing I understand."

"Can we cast a spell to sniff out the source?" Lionel asked.

"Is this rash normal?" Bramble asked.

Agnes moved around the body to see what Bramble pointed at. A rash ran down the side of the body, large blisters with darker blue surrounding them. "The medical examiner might be able to tell you, but don't go closer in case it's contagious."

"No," Bramble said. "I won't touch it, but it is dead, whatever it is."

If he can tell by just looking, maybe the CDC should start hiring fairies.

"What about a spell?" Lionel asked again.

"What would you cast?" Agnes asked. She wasn't sure they should be doing any magic before the body went to the morgue for autopsy, but she was interested in learning as much as she could about how they would use it.

"There are a few I can think of," Lionel answered. "We could try to recreate the scene, like a movie of what happened. That will help unless someone has blocked it. I know several spells designed specifically to find the presence of different spell ingredients, but I probably need to go back to my workshop to access the components."

The body twitched again, causing Agnes to jump.

"Do you want to leave?" Mamoru asked. "It's unsettling."

Why did he keep trying to protect her? "This is more than unsettling. It's horrifying. I will stay until we are all ready to leave."

"Not magic, or not anything we would do," Bramble said

as he flew back to join them. "Maybe someone made the drug again? A human. Someone who doesn't understand magic."

"It's definitely magic," Agnes said. "Nothing natural would make the body move like that."

"Bugs," Bramble said. "Maybe someone put bugs under his skin."

"No bug I know can move a dead body," Agnes said.

"Fine, it is magic," Bramble said. "I meant it isn't one of us magical folk. Why would we do something so awful?"

Fernlight moved toward the body, shaking her head. "No human can do magic, Bramble. Stop pretending it couldn't be one of the magical folk."

"How about a spell?" Lionel asked again. "At least we can confirm who was here."

"A rogue wizard!" Bramble exclaimed. "Remember, Fernlight? When we first opened our agency. Thorn said there were rumors about one."

"Wizards don't go rogue," Lionel said.

Agnes wondered how they could be so sure. Uncertainty about what a magical person was capable of was the basis of most of the fear generated by these folk. People, human people, thought they understood even the most extreme motives. They thought being human made you similar to them. When magical folk didn't value what a human would value, it made them unpredictable.

She knew this scene was going to leave her with nightmares. Mamoru was pale and kept his eye averted from the body. Human reactions. The three magical folk didn't seem to be affected emotionally in any way.

"There's no point in guessing," she said. "I think any spells you need to cast should wait for the medical examiner and the crime scene team. When the scene has been processed, I would like to see what your spells can do. Before that, we run the risk of having the evidence called into question because of magic."

"I will take one more look around," Bramble said. "If there are clues up in the ceiling, I can tell the humans to look for them. Is that okay?"

Mamoru called Bramble back. "Do you have your phone?"

"No, Fernlight is holding it. I can use it to take pictures, right? That is a very good idea, Mamoru." He took the phone from Fernlight and sped to the ceiling.

Agnes looked at the body again. The movement was still frenzied. "If magic can do this, how will we ever solve a case without it?"

"That's the entire point we've been trying to make," Fernlight said.

"Then you should welcome my participation," Agnes said. "Please remember this is all new to us. We don't have a long list of unsolved cases that are probably magic crimes to base our future rulings on. Our legal system works on precedent. We will be creating new processes every time you cast a spell or use a charm. I am not the enemy."

"I understand," Fernlight said. "Please remember we also have no history of this kind of thing. No long list of crimes, solved or unsolved. Before the prophecy, the magical folk didn't commit murder."

CHAPTER FOUR

Bramble was glad to be out of the room. The body got more disturbing as time passed and the jerking didn't stop. If magic made the movement happen, he couldn't sense it. That was the most difficult part. If there was a rogue wizard with magic that could hide, no one would be safe.

"The spell to show what happened would not have changed anything about the evidence," he said.

He liked Agnes. She seemed to understand the problem and some kinds of magic. But she should let them do what they needed to do.

"It's not that, Bramble," Lionel said. "The humans don't trust us."

"That's not correct," Mamoru said. "I realize we are all upset about what we just witnessed, but that is not an excuse to keep arguing the same points over and over. The courts need to be sure nothing you do influences the outcome."

Are we upset? Bramble fluttered around the group. Yes, he saw worry all over Lionel's face. Fernlight was fading again, like she'd been using power to keep calm. Not even the humans were really fine with the dancing body. He didn't know the man, so why would he spend time feeling bad?

"We must not waste time," he said. "I am very glad my children were not here because they have not seen so many bad things as I have. But this case must be solved quickly. Heath's murderer is still walking around free and might be preparing to kill another wizard." Quinn Larson's image floated into his mind. It would be awful if he died. And Lionel. He didn't know any other wizards.

"Taking a moment to accept the facts is not wasting time," Fernlight said. "We need to be able to think clearly. Just because we don't know the victim doesn't mean we can dismiss our feelings. And perhaps we do know him. The body was damaged so it could be anyone."

"Human. Anyone human," Bramble reminded them. "And we know magic was involved. And the magic is bad if it keeps going when the person is dead."

"Does magic fail if the person casting it dies?" Agnes asked.

"If they die, or if the victim of the spell dies. This is not normal," Lionel said. "Some old and powerful spells can rebound to the caster if they kill the victim. It's why we put our spells in charms. Helps to contain them."

A charm? Bramble buzzed back into the room. He didn't even think of looking for one. It made all kinds of sense. He heard Mamoru calling but ignored him. This would only take one second, two at the most. And he was wearing the stupid suit.

He sniffed the air, but the smell of the dead man was too dense. He closed his eyes and let his mind think about charms. Yes, there was something nearby. He would warn Mamoru, maybe they should make the brownies help search for things. A good way to keep them occupied and out of his way.

He flew back and reported. "Now can I get out of these clothes? I am hot inside here."

Mamoru led them back to the room where the box of suits sat. Seven humans were waiting for their turn to go in. Bramble peeled the suit off like a skin and flew to the first human. "There is a charm inside. I couldn't tell where. You must be careful what you touch."

The woman looked to Mamoru. "How are we supposed to deal with that?"

"To be completely safe, be careful about any objects that don't seem to fit. Lionel, can you help?"

"The charm is probably a lump of stone or a gem. Or maybe a seed or a pinecone or something like that. I'm sorry I can't be more specific. Perhaps I should accompany you?"

The woman shook her head. "We'll be careful."

Outside on the street, Bramble suggested they send the brownies to help.

"After the team has done their work," Mamoru said. "You can ask them to wait out here, but it will be hours."

"Brownies are not that patient," Bramble said. "Your team should be safe. We're wasting time again."

"Bramble, you must know solving a crime takes time," Agnes said. "I understand you are worried about finding your friend's killer, but rushing won't help. I promise I will work as fast as I can to get approval on the use of at least some magic."

He did like her, but she didn't know how it felt. He wanted to catch the person who ordered Heath to be killed before his own death. The oldest fairies he knew of died at six and he was four years old already.

CHAPTER FIVE

Bramble felt both safe and annoyed being in the office. Safe because everyone there was part of the team and annoyed because every investigation kept him inside when he was certain answers lay outside. But until he knew what questions to ask, and who to ask, he would stick with the safety of his desk and the computer that held so many wonderful things.

"What do we do now?" he asked Mamoru. "How long will those people take at the crime scene? How soon can we see the body? What if it is still dancing? Will the medical examiner be able to explain why?"

"A lot of questions," Mamoru said. "I am not sure what the next step is. We will know more when we receive the results. The crime scene team will be hours yet. The body will be with the medical examiner soon. I asked him to inform us when he is ready to start so we can be there. And I have no idea about the movement."

"You should allow the brownies to help," Lionel said. "They can look into the smallest cracks, and there are so many of them, it might only take an hour to do the job. Maybe less."

Bramble was about to agree when Agnes stood from where she'd been sitting on the edge of a desk.

Great. Now she will say that magical creatures are not allowed to help. It would mean the brownies could go away, but they would be helpful and that was more important than how annoying they were.

"What skills do the brownies have?" she asked.

Bramble was ready to say they were sneaky and untrustworthy, as well as dirty, when Lionel answered. "They are very good at finding things. They have organizational skills and since there are so many of them in the horde, they can cover a variety of tasks at the same time."

Agnes thanked Lionel and said, "I need to talk to them. Can you bring them here? I need to understand how they go about finding things. If I can justify their methods, I think everyone would be happy to have the crime scene examination go faster."

"I suppose we can add that to your remit," Mamoru said. "But even if you are happy with them, I'm not sure if there are small enough suits."

"Remember, I can create a spell to keep all their contamination inside," Lionel said. "Your human team might appreciate not being inside those outfits."

"A magical solution will need to be tested," Agnes said. "But if it passes, you will gain a lot of fans."

Testing! Delays again.

"We are busy right now with a task from Kim," Pit said.

"How long have you been here?" Bramble would ask Lionel for a spell that would warn them when brownies were lurking, perhaps a bell they could wear.

"From before you returned," Pit said. "We would be very happy to help and if you can show us one of these suits, we will tell you if we can make them fit." He turned to Agnes. "I am Pit, and this is my horde."

"Pleased to meet you," Agnes said. "You are quite small."

She bent to talk to Pit, but even as low as she could get, she was still many times taller than the brownie leader.

"We can shrink many things," Pit said. "Not everything. We will be available to talk to you this afternoon. Is that convenient?"

He was just trying to make himself important, Bramble thought. Before he could say anything, Pit disappeared under Lionel's desk. Kim did not volunteer the information on the task she'd asked them to do, so it was probably something Mamoru shouldn't hear.

"Someone is calling you," Fernlight said to Mamoru.

He checked his phone.

"No, not that way. Through a circle," she said.

Mamoru is nervous! He swallowed when Fernlight said circle. He hadn't been in one ever. Maybe he thought that every time would be like when the bad man, Talbot Ryce, talked back to them. "It's safe," he said, patting Mamoru's shoulder. "I will make sure you are not harmed."

"Thank you," Mamoru said. "I am simply wondering if it is appropriate for me to communicate in this manner." He looked at Agnes, and Bramble thought he hoped she would say no.

"I think it is an excellent chance for me to experience magic," Agnes said. "And, I assume this has nothing to do with the case, so I don't need to assess the effects. I am looking forward to it."

"Then let's get it over with," Mamoru said. "My last encounter with magic was not pleasant."

He was thinking about when Kali possessed him five years ago. "A communication circle will not be like that," Bramble said, trying to sound kind but was not sure if he managed. "I promise."

Fernlight made the windows of the outer office so people

couldn't see in, and then set the circle to include four people. It was a squish and Bramble had to keep his wings in check, but maybe the conversation wouldn't be long.

"Who calls us to the circle?" Fernlight asked when everyone was seated.

"Mamoru will come to the court to speak to me in person," Maeve's voice said.

"We are in the middle of an important case," Bramble said. He would not be pushed around by a sidhe, queen or not. He was a king and that made them equals. And she wasn't here, so it was safe.

"It is critical that I meet with you," Maeve said. "Do not bring the fairy."

The connection cut off.

Fernlight broke the circle but no one moved.

"She cannot tell us what to do," Bramble said. "She does not rule us. She hasn't sent a sidhe to join the team."

"What if she has information about the body?" Agnes asked. "We shouldn't ignore something she thinks is critical."

"She doesn't know what that means," Bramble said. The look on her face told him he'd almost hit the fairy range of sound. He told his voice to behave and started again. "It will be about something important to Maeve, not to anyone else."

"We won't be sure until we listen to what she wants to say," Agnes said. "If it is not important to our case, we will politely decline to help."

Bramble couldn't keep his anger alive when she used such a gentle voice. "It's a good thing I'm not going."

CHAPTER SIX

"I will take only two others," Mamoru said. "Lionel? I believe you are known to Maeve?"

Known isn't what I would label it.

"I've been to court a few times," he said. "I have no problems with the sidhe court at this time." He hoped that would remain true. Being part of the team with Mamoru solidified his position as an actual investigator. Since he'd joined, Lionel sat at the computer. Now Kim would do that, and he would be in the field.

Mamoru didn't seem to notice his excitement because he turned to Kim. She sat with Raj, the new human recruit. If Kim came, Lionel would be the least qualified detective. But that was true no matter who Mamoru picked.

"Mr. Mander, is your induction finished?"

"Call me Raj," the new man said. "I think Kim's finished. I'm happy to join you. Never seen more than one sidhe."

"Then both of you will join me."

Lionel pushed out his chair, ready to leave.

"Mamoru," Fernlight said, "I may need them on the case.

If someone contacts us, I want the full complement to draw from."

Lionel stopped moving. Would Mamoru change his mind? He understood Fernlight's concerns, but this was his opportunity.

"I am only taking two people to minimize the impact on your team. If you need them, please don't hesitate to call me and end our meeting with Maeve. But you do understand that the queen holds political influence. We cannot ignore her."

"I think we can make this fast," Lionel said. "Mamoru, I'm not sure the phone will work in the court. I will make sure we are not stuck accepting any invitations to stay."

"It is not that," Fernlight said. "I don't know how human teams work, but I thought Bramble and I were the leaders here, yet Mamoru is choosing team members."

Lionel didn't answer. Not because he was afraid; this was between Fernlight and Mamoru. If they were at odds, it didn't take a genius to know the detective agency would fall apart.

"I apologize," Mamoru said. "I am not used to working with people who don't really report to me. What do you suggest?"

Fernlight accepted the apology. "You chose the right people. Heed Lionel, both of you. If you accept an invitation to dine with the sidhe, we will not see you until tomorrow and even then, you will be in no condition to think straight. We cannot afford to lose anyone for that long."

Lionel joined the two humans at the door. "It would be better if I did the speaking," he said, "but Maeve might not let us decide."

"Why don't you call her Queen Maeve?" Raj asked.

Lionel took a look at him before answering. Raj was tall, and despite his body being slender, he was a little paunchy but still good looking. He wore a bright blue turban, black jacket, white shirt, black pants and shoes. His clothes would work for the court. Mamoru was impeccably dressed in a dark suit as usual. Lionel admitted to himself that he was the only one who might not be acceptably turned out. Jeans, a teeshirt and runners. It was a good thing that Maeve knew him.

"In the court and to gain access, we use her title," he said, "but she is not our queen, so we use her name when not addressing her. The same way we don't call Bramble king."

"Bramble is a king?" Raj asked. "He seems…"

"When he is with his people, or other fairies, he is a king." Lionel pushed the door open. "We should go. Please remember to be respectful when you are talking to any of the sidhe in or around the court. They can be very obstructive if they take offense."

He noticed a smile cross Mamoru's face. Perhaps he'd already had dealings with the court.

"Isn't one of the team a sidhe?" Raj asked as they strode toward Yaletown, where the court currently hid.

"That's one thing I'd like to clear up with Maeve in the meeting," Mamoru said. "She has not yet sent anyone to join us."

It doesn't matter. If she's changed her mind, nothing Mamoru can say will change it back.

CHAPTER SEVEN

"If you are offered food or drink, it's okay to accept or decline," Lionel said as they walked the corridor surrounding the court, the sounds of the traffic outside in Yaletown muted to near silence. One of the twins who guarded the door was leading them, and unlike the first few times Lionel had attended court, they hadn't threatened or insulted anyone. "But please don't accept any invitations. I will do the talking unless Maeve actually speaks to one of you."

The two humans kept silent, so he could only hope there would be no unrecoverable mistakes. They were escorted directly to the queen's seat. The court was currently decorated in decadent French style. Lionel didn't care for it, but he exclaimed at the sight as soon as Maeve finished the introductions.

"I didn't call you here to talk about decorations. I need your services, Mr. Yamana." Maeve's voice was still musical and soft, but her agitation came as a surprise.

"I am happy to provide people if you know of a crime to be investigated," Mamoru said. "Perhaps you can explain the problem."

Too blunt.

Maeve didn't react. "Are you aware that I am working with the new minister for magical affairs to build a set of guidelines on how to integrate the humans with the magical world?"

Please don't argue. Lionel expected Mamoru to say it was the other way around. The magical world needed to integrate with the human one. But he gave a slight bow of his head and gestured for her to continue.

"He is missing. I tried to locate him using a tracker spell with no success. I want your team to take the investigation." She waved to one of her attendants. "Bring wine, and some of those sweet pastries."

"I have many investigators," Mamoru said. "If you can give me the details, I will assign the correct team. There will be interest from the political side too. The RCMP will be involved."

"I don't care what you have to do," Maeve said. "You must assign some of the investigators from Lionel's team."

Mamoru's expression was blank. He must be very good at dealing with the political aspects of his job, Lionel thought. Although he might not like being told how to use his investigators, he didn't argue. "It is probable that they are the best team," he said.

"This must be a priority," Maeve said. She waved her attendant to offer the refreshments around. No one accepted. "I will not allow rumors to be spread that people dealing with the sidhe are not safe."

"No one would think that," Lionel said. "I'm sure it is simply a case of him leaving for a holiday, or a short break, or a meeting."

"I thought you were smarter than that, Lionel. His staff are not aware of any of those. And if it is innocent, how do you explain the failure of the tracker?"

He imagined that if Maeve was as demanding as usual with the minister, the man would have found a charm to confuse a tracker. They weren't easy to get, but who knows what contacts he had in the magical world.

"Have you informed the authorities?" Mamoru asked before Lionel found the words to answer Maeve's question.

"I have no interest in your rules, Mr. Yamana. I trust his staff to take care of such matters."

"When we receive the information, I will talk to Fernlight about the best team," Mamoru said.

"You will make this a high priority and you will assign your best investigators." Maeve's voice was cold.

"Of course," Lionel said. He took a step to put Mamoru a little behind him. Thank goodness Raj seemed overawed by the sidhe and kept his mouth shut. "I think we all agree this is of the utmost importance. Perhaps you can give Leith the details and he can present them when he arrives at the office?"

"Yes, perhaps Leith would be the best to lead the investigation," Maeve said.

Lionel couldn't be sure if she was serious, or just being obstructive to Mamoru. She couldn't be enjoying the fact she needed to ask for help; the entire conversation had been completely without courtly manners. But if she wanted Leith to lead the team, she intended to use him as a spy. That could not happen. Time to make a little space for thought.

"Perhaps we should call Fernlight to discuss?" he asked. "We certainly want to use Leith in the best cases. That would shine a favorable light on the sidhe, after all."

"I think, perhaps I should have called Fernlight to me. I thought you were in charge…Mr. Yamana."

Lionel heard contempt in her voice. She had almost called him human rather than his name. Maeve was rattled.

"This team is contracted to HOP-D," Mamoru said. "A

call to Fernlight and Bramble would be politically right." He pulled out his phone.

"You will need to leave to make your call. Those devices do not work inside the court."

Mamoru motioned for Raj and Lionel to join him outside.

"Wait, leave the young human here. It will ensure you return to collect him without delay. And he seems to properly appreciate the company."

"It would be best for him to join us," Lionel said.

"I'll be fine," Raj said. "I have aunties who could give lessons in intimidation to this lovely queen." He smiled as he spoke and bowed to Maeve. "I would be honored to learn more about you."

The smile did it. Lionel saw Maeve's appreciation of the way it seemed to be just for her. Like they had a secret. Lionel wondered if Raj would be willing to give him lessons on how to impress the opposite sex.

CHAPTER EIGHT

The street was busy, and Lionel needed privacy to reach out. "I could slip into the alley," he said to Mamoru.

"First let me make a few calls. I assume we cannot take all day for this. How long will Maeve wait?"

Lionel considered. Maeve was impatient. But she had a new toy in Raj. "Unless Raj is highly entertaining, we should probably take no more than fifteen minutes. But who else is she going to call to help?"

Mamoru pressed a button on his phone. "She has investigated before. We want Leith on our team, not competing with us."

He turned his attention to the person on the other end of the call, and Lionel waited. He wanted to help, but even five years after the humans learned about the magical world, no magical person would cast a circle in public. The humans would not know better than to barge through the salt and break the protections, unleashing all kinds of mayhem.

"Lionel?" Mamoru was looking at him.

"I was thinking," Lionel said. No need to tell him it was about the circle. "Did you find out anything?"

"No one official is talking," Mamoru said. "I have a contact who is less official and more obliging. Is there any way you can cast that privacy spell? If he hears street noise, I will not be able to get anything from him."

"It might block your signal, but we can try." He pulled Mamoru, gently and respectfully, into the shade of a bricked-up doorway. "Don't move around. The spell is very narrow. If I make it bigger, someone could enter by mistake."

Mamoru nodded and pressed another button. "Limpid."

"Why did you hang up?" Lionel looked at the phone. Yes, the call was definitely ended. "And what does limpid mean?"

"He is paranoid. There is actually no one after him. I checked thoroughly. It's a code word and he will call back from an untraceable number, and we'll see if he knows anything."

"If he is so secretive, how does he learn things to help?" Lionel wondered if this person should be part of their team.

"He keeps his identity hidden. He does not hide himself. He works, he has friends. No one is sure of his alternate identity. Not even me. I have never met him. Or perhaps I have."

The phone rang.

"Thank you for calling back," Mamoru said, holding the phone between them.

"What do you want?" the voice was a bland, electronic version of English.

"What do you know about the minister for magical affairs?"

"You messing in magic?"

Mamoru looked at Lionel as if telling him to keep silent, but Lionel had no intention of making any noise.

"I run a team of detectives," Mamoru said. "If you don't know that, maybe I'm wasting my time."

"Just testing, Buddy. Maybe I can get hooked up with them? Learn a few tricks. Buy one of those glamour things?"

"I can see how that would help, but you would need to reveal yourself," Mamoru said. "Are you prepared to do that?"

"I heard they got oaths that they can't break. But you didn't call about that. Your minister has been missing for a few days. No one wants to admit it, or officially report it, but inside they are panicking. You going to tell your fairies to find him?"

"Not only fairies." Mamoru looked at Lionel again. "Anything else?"

"No. Give your team the same number and tell them to use the code squishy." The call ended.

"So, Maeve was telling the truth." Lionel lifted the spell. "At least the truth that she wants to share."

"When we go back, we need to make sure Leith is headed for the office by the end of the day and that he isn't going to be assigned to Maeve's investigation. We need to start as we intend to continue — we choose the investigators, not her."

"Okay. You want me to tell her?" Lionel hoped his reluctance didn't show on his face.

"No. Just don't do anything that might give her an edge. Now I understand why Fernlight is so unhappy with me. I shall strive to be better."

Lionel laughed at the idea that Maeve would simply comply. They crossed the road and passed through the guards into the court.

"Are you going to give Fernlight the phone number?"

"I need to think it through," Mamoru said. He straightened his already perfect suit jacket. "He is difficult to handle. When I do, I want to be sure Fernlight and Bramble know what they are in for with him."

The inner court doors opened. Lionel followed Mamoru through and came to a stop. Raj stood beside Maeve, a look of adoration on his face. She had him under a compulsion. How could she betray their trust so much?

CHAPTER NINE

Lionel swallowed his immediate reaction and turned to Mamoru. "Do not try to get him away from Maeve. I will deal with this."

Mamoru followed Lionel to the queen's inner circle. There were several ways to break a compulsion, but none of them left the subject unaltered. If Maeve wanted their cooperation, she shouldn't play so freely with the investigators. This would damage any relationship she'd built with the humans. And not just them. Bramble would be insufferable in pointing out he was right about sidhe.

He slowed his pace as other thoughts nudged aside the anger. Maeve ran the court, not Fionuir. Maeve wasn't impulsive. That meant Raj had done something to offend. A different problem to solve.

"Your majesty," he said with a bow. "I can only apologize for whatever caused you to bespell our companion."

He tried to keep his eyes on Maeve, but Raj started vibrating. It was worse than he imagined. A grin broke the man's face, and everyone around them laughed.

"Raj, that was amusing," Maeve said, "although I fear you will have amends to make."

A joke? How could he play a joke on them? This was a dangerous way to act with the sidhe.

"Humorous," Mamoru said. "But if we are to solve the case, we should not waste time. I have received confirmation that the minister is gone, but no other details seem available."

"I expect you to make it a priority," Maeve said, still smiling.

"When will Leith report to the agency?" Mamoru asked, carefully not responding to her comment.

"He will be there today." She looked away, appearing bored with the conversation.

Of course she is, Lionel thought. As soon as the details of investigating her case started, she slid her attention to something else. He shifted his weight, hoping Mamoru would let him take over.

"Very well," Mamoru said. "And what other assistance will we receive from you or your court?" It seemed that Mamoru knew exactly what he was doing.

"Leith will be my contact," she said. "Anything you need, please inform him. I will expect him to report frequently."

"He may not be assigned to the case," Mamoru said. "It would be prudent to have a more flexible form of communication."

And now they were at the key point of the conversation. If Maeve trusted them, she was only testing the boundaries. If she didn't, then Mamoru would not get his way.

Maeve called for more wine. She addressed a few sidhe who stood nearby to arrange some of the articles on a table across the court.

Lionel looked toward the table and saw Ailin. Attacked by the synymphs years ago, he still wore the scars. The fact that Maeve did not allow him to heal the damage or use a glamour to cover the disfigurement was a message in itself. Fail and you will suffer the consequences. Mamoru wouldn't understand. This message was for Lionel.

Maeve finally turned back to the waiting humans. "I trust you to manage your resources. Raj, you are welcome in my court anytime. Please do not make yourself a stranger."

"It would be a pleasure to come again. The case will probably take my time for the next few days, but I promise to return before you forget inviting me." He bowed low and turned on his heel.

Mamoru made the rest of the goodbyes and left after receiving a charm to communicate with Maeve.

They stood on the street moments later. Lionel couldn't let the worry about Maeve's message slip away.

"Why did that one sidhe look so different?" Mamoru asked. "All the others were flawless, he was..."

"Flawed," Lionel finished the sentence. "He rebelled and harmed a lot of other magical folk. Maeve punished him by removing his protections for a day. Those claw marks happened within a few seconds."

"It's like they paraded him out for us as a warning," Raj said. "Like when the aunties tell the kids about cousin Yafir and his time in jail."

"Should we be concerned, Lionel?" Mamoru asked. "I don't plan to purposely offend her, but I think that might be impossible to avoid."

Lionel turned back to look at the entrance to the court, thinking.

It is never about one thing with the sidhe.

"Maeve meant it as a warning to me," he said. "I was the only non-sidhe there who knew the story. But I think I am expected to pass it on to the team. If we don't solve the case fast, she will act."

"Then we will proceed quickly," Mamoru said.

"Good thing she likes me," Raj said.

"A warning to you, too." Lionel reached to press the button to stop traffic. "She knew I would tell you the story. Ailin was a favorite of the court at one time. Be careful, Raj. She won't always find you funny."

Raj paled and then grinned. He recovered too fast for Lionel to think him serious. "Don't worry, Lionel. I told you; I grew up with the aunties. I know how to manage women who think they own you."

"I hope so," Lionel said.

The light changed, the traffic stopped, and they started walking back to the office.

CHAPTER TEN

Agnes sat at the back of the room and observed. It wasn't strictly in her remit to assess the team dynamics, but she found them fascinating. They reacted faster than an all-human team. Was it just the way magical people worked, or was it because bureaucracy and habit didn't bog them down?

Perhaps she would talk to Kim later to get closer to the truth or ask for an opinion she could understand — human to human.

"I am only offering a suggestion," Mamoru said to Fernlight. "It is based on the information available and my experience."

The sprite was defensive about leading the group. Bramble, who was supposed to be the co-leader, seemed more concerned about which case he would be investigating. If they asked her, Agnes would suggest that both teams have magical and non-magical investigators. Starting with that approach would do more to advance the use of magic than keeping the humans together.

She looked around the room. Most of the people waited for a decision. The brownies peeking out from under Lionel's desk were paying close attention. Kim was talking to the sidhe investigator. The rest clustered around a computer, hopefully starting their research.

"We should all speak," Bramble announced. "This is a team. We do not report to HOP-D. We are consultants."

They were sensitive, Agnes knew. HOP-D had a well-deserved reputation for bias against magical beings. It was possible her work would help them believe in the benefit of magic as an investigative tool.

Fernlight and Mamoru stood side by side. Perhaps Mamoru didn't realize the message that sent about leadership — or perhaps he did it on purpose.

"We have two cases," Fernlight said.

"Three," Bramble said, reminding them of Heath's murder. "It's not solved until we catch the human behind that woman."

"But two active ones," Mamoru said. "The murder and the missing minister take precedence."

"Yes," Bramble said. "I will work on the murder. It is magical, and it might be the same person who ordered Heath's death."

Mamoru didn't say anything.

"Leith will join me and Bramble," Fernlight said. "We need magical expertise."

"I will not stay in the office again," Lionel said. He seemed nervous and didn't look at Fernlight.

"Someone must coordinate the work," Mamoru said. "I will take updates from that person. It allows you to continue without interruptions."

"Look," Kim said, "we're wasting time arguing. I'll stay in the office. I can coordinate the information. I know how to update daily. I can work with the brownies unless you want them on a team?"

"And my children," Bramble said. "These are very dangerous cases. I want them here."

"And the kids. Both teams are going to need information and research. I will make sure it's available." The way Kim said research made Agnes more determined to talk to her.

"Since you are worried that I will be Queen Maeve's spy," Leith said, his voice smooth and urbane, "I will join the murder team."

Maybe she imagined the tension earlier. Agnes waited to see what would happen with Raj. Since they only had one human to add to an investigation, and a new team member to boot, would they try to leave him in the office?

Mamoru seemed to know what she was thinking because he looked at the three remaining team members. Then, turning to her, he asked, "Agnes, which team will you shadow?"

It was good to get his assumptions into the light. "I will follow both teams. I will decide where I am best placed to assess magic, and perhaps to provide some guidance."

She didn't mention that she would also be looking at the work the brownies and fairy children did.

"Then Lionel and I will take Maeve's case," Rhodri, a druid who she'd met earlier, said. "It may not be more than a mundane missing person's case. I think we can handle that."

"And me?" Raj asked. "I'm not used to getting a choice."

"You should take him on the murder," Agnes said. She didn't know why the words came out, but something had urged her to speak. Her intuition had served well in the past; she chose to trust it now.

Fernlight looked at Raj and then Bramble. Of course, fairies feared humans and she didn't want it affecting the investigation.

"Yes," Bramble said. "I will not be afraid of him. He is like Kim, one of our team. And we get to see how he works. And if you say Maeve likes you, it's probably best that you don't work on her case."

"Who will be our team leader?" Lionel asked. "I mean, we will work as a team, obviously, but one of us should be given the last word in a dispute, right?"

Rhodri moved closer to Lionel. "We will work that out as we go."

No one offered any other suggestions. Agnes had no interest in getting involved with the initial planning. She looked to the brownies to ask about their methods.

They were gone.

CHAPTER ELEVEN

"What will we do first?" Bramble hovered at Fernlight's elbow. "Lionel and Rhodri can figure out the first step, but I don't know where to start. Will we get to see the body?"

"Before you start, I want to be clear," Mamoru said. "You will cooperate with Agnes."

If she is asleep, we won't have to wake her up.

"You will not dodge her or use a sleep spell."

So, we can always tell her something to keep her away, like we aren't going to do magic.

"You will not lie to her; you will not turn her into a toad."

Bramble heard chuckles and noticed Agnes laughing. *They will not think it funny when she gets in the way.*

"We will treat her honorably," Rhodri said. "It is to our benefit to give her every opportunity to understand how magic will help in an investigation."

Druids. They drained the fun out of everything.

Mamoru nodded. "We will leave you to your work. Agnes needs to complete some training and then she will return."

Fernlight nudged Bramble. How did she know he was

going to say something? "Will we be able to examine the body again?"

Mamoru nodded. "The medical examiner will contact you when he is ready."

"Until he does," Raj said, "we can research the owner of the building. Perhaps there will be security cameras. Or perhaps the owner can identify our victim."

It was good to have an experienced investigator on the team, Bramble thought. "Yes. What kind of training will Agnes get?" If it was anything to do with magic, she should do her lessons with them. What did HOP-D know about magic? They would tell her magic was a bad tool, not a good one. And they thought magical folk were bad, so that wouldn't help.

"We have some security steps," Mamoru said. "We will show her how to enter her findings into the HOP-D system. I will brief her on your last few cases and the magic that I am aware you used."

He knew they kept some things secret! "What magic?" The team would need to be very careful about using magic that Agnes didn't learn about ahead of time. Would she tell Mamoru if she found a spell that he didn't know about? Would this be worse than he feared?

"Tracking spells," Mamoru said. "I believe you also used magic to restrain people. You used magic to resolve the case with Talbot Ryce, so nothing became contaminated."

"Yes. Those were all used to help the case." Bramble was relieved. Mamoru didn't count the use of magic folk. People like Nitro and other house fairies. Or the spell to call the spider. Or the spells to open locks.

"I'm sure you will show her the others," Mamoru said with a smile. "She can advise you on the best way to search a home or office."

He knew about the invisibility spells!

"I'm sure there are many more that will be of use," Mamoru said. "We'll leave you now."

Agnes said she'd be back and followed Mamoru through the door.

"You can enter houses without picking a lock?" Raj asked. "Or did I misunderstand?"

"How do humans do it?" Bramble asked. He wasn't ready to trust Raj. But if humans went into places uninvited, magic wouldn't make any difference.

"I use a set of lock picks. They kind of work like a key," Raj answered. "The whole process can take a couple of minutes. And sometimes you leave a few scratches. That's not great."

"I have not heard of a spell to open locks," Leith said. "They are too complicated for one spell. Add to that a security system and you basically need to create a separate spell for each lock. However, we wouldn't leave scratches. And after an hour or so, no one would sense that magic had been done."

Maybe no sidhe could do it!

"Fairies have very sophisticated magic," Bramble said. He would go no further. If the sidhe needed to know the spell, he would ask. If he was too proud to ask, then he would not learn anything. And maybe Bramble would not be willing to tell him anyway. Fairy magic was for fairies.

"I look forward to seeing you in action," Leith said with a bow. "Now I think it is time to plan our investigation."

"Yes." Bramble flitted to a whiteboard. "First, I want to say that we should not forget about Heath. If we can't find information on the dancing body, perhaps we should try to figure out more about Heath's murderer."

CHAPTER TWELVE

Bramble moved closer to Raj. He would rather sit with a human than with the sidhe.

"I think we all need to talk about this," Fernlight said. "Both investigations need a plan and, like Bramble keeps reminding us, we don't have a satisfactory end to Heath's murder."

"Perhaps you can tell us a little about the history of Heath's murder," Leith said. "I am not the only one who wasn't here last week."

He should have learned that before he came, Bramble thought. "Heath got murdered and we found out who actually killed him, but she said she was just doing what someone else told her to do. We don't know who ordered her to kill our friend. We won't be happy until that person is punished."

"There's a bit more to it than that," Fernlight said. "But it's enough for now. We are working two official cases and one that Mamoru seems to think is unimportant."

Bramble watched the sidhe to make sure he wasn't going to argue. This was too important to let Leith confuse everything.

"You haven't assigned anyone to Heath's case," Raj said. "I'm all for a little secret work, but if we have to hide it from Mamoru, it's going to be hard with Agnes watching us."

"Yes," Bramble said. "Someone needs to keep her busy. I like her, but she won't let us do what we need to."

Kim stood and stepped out from behind her desk. "Don't get in her way. The faster she does her job, the better. I think we need to look at the information we do know before we rush off."

"That's what I'm trying to do here," Fernlight said. Then she laughed. "Working with a team is different from adding a few people to the company."

"You have that board," Leith said. "Perhaps we can use it to list what we currently know and how we can use the information?"

"Yes. We do that with investigations," Bramble said. "If you stop interrupting, we can get on with it." Leith gave him a nod like Bramble needed permission to go ahead.

Lionel took the pen from Fernlight and wrote the three cases on the board, leaving room to add information under the headings. "Let's stop arguing and do it. I'm looking forward to solving my first case, so Rhodri and I need to start."

Fernlight took the pen and wrote names under the two cases. "We should all work on Heath's case when we have time," she said. "These are the investigators. Kim and the brownies and kids will work research and support on all three. What do we know about Heath's murder case?"

"He was killed by someone important," Bramble said. "He spent all his time working on making magic tools for everyone to use. He found out that someone wanted to use his magic tools to make war. He refused. They killed him."

Fernlight added the points under the heading. She added what they knew about the other two cases as well.

"I was acquainted with Heath. I may have more details for you," Leith said. "He was working with Maeve to find a way around the damping effect of the court. She wanted to be able to use a phone and to search this Internet thing everyone loves."

"Did she order another sidhe to kill him?" Bramble asked.

"No," Leith said. "She asked me to look into his death too. He moved here from a place called Boston. He has wanted to help humans since the prophecy revealed our world to them. He had what turned out to be an unhealthy passion for efficiency."

"How does that help?" Bramble asked. *Why were the others just listening?*

"Knowing your victim is important," Kim said. "If you understand their lives, you might find the connection to the killer. Is there a way to track who he talked to in his circles?"

"Like a magical call log?" Raj asked. "Would he have been able to talk to a human in the circle?"

That was a better way to use the time, Bramble thought. "Maybe. If he sent them a salt string and they agreed on what time to connect." He thought for a second longer. "But I don't think anyone we worked with in the previous investigations understood circles. So, it doesn't help us."

"But is there a way?" Kim asked again.

"Let me look into it," Rhodri said. "There isn't much knowledge about how humans interact with us, but maybe one of my brothers at the grove will have researched the topic."

It was a new thing at least. Bramble wanted this case solved before he died. Fairies seemed to live longer now, but he was old and didn't know how long he had to solve cases.

"So, we don't really have anything to follow up on," Leith said. "Something might turn up in the research, but I don't see a starting point."

"Not unusual," Fernlight said. "We should keep this information up to date. When we find something to follow up on, we'll do it. Right now, the dancing body and the missing minister cases have actions for us to take. We need to be ready to go to the autopsy, and Lionel and Rhodri need to interview the minister's employees and family."

"I suppose we can do some research while we wait for Mamoru to call," Leith said. "Perhaps we can locate some of Heath's inventions in this Internet."

Bramble didn't know what to say to that. It was a good idea, but he still didn't trust the sidhe. Perhaps saying nothing would be better.

"Bramble, can I talk to you privately?" Fernlight asked.

The others went back to their computers to start searching for information. Bramble took one more look at the board before joining her in the outer office. She cast a privacy spell and then said, "Are you going to fight Leith every step of the way through this?"

"What? I was polite, but he didn't need to keep interrupting and slowing us down. He should listen more than he talks."

"Even when you didn't argue, it was clear you wanted to. Every time he speaks, you frown at him. Everyone can tell you don't want him here."

"I don't. So, can we send him back to Maeve?"

"He is an investigator. She will order him to work on the minister case and he will get in the way. She will not restrict his use of magic and that will work against us. I think he's a good team member. You need to give him a chance."

"But he is a sidhe. If you trust him, you will be sorry." *How did she not know that?*

"I am familiar with the sidhe. If we are going to convince humans to trust us, do you think it might help if we at least looked like we trust each other?"

"Only look like?"

"And act like it. I'm not saying trust him, but make everyone believe you do. All the magical folk in that room are aware of the way sidhe think. All of us are on guard."

He thought they'd forgotten all the history of the sidhe making plots and betraying people. "You are all doing a very good job of pretending," he said. "I will do the same."

Fernlight released the spell and ushered him back to the team. He smiled at everyone including Leith. It was going to be a big effort to pretend, but he understood the importance. He never thought he would work with sidhe or brownies, but this was a new world for everyone.

CHAPTER THIRTEEN

Finally, something was happening on the case. Bramble tried to keep his wings under control because they wanted to go faster than the others could move. They were going to the morgue to see the body and talk to the special human who would listen to them about the magic part.

"It's going to be difficult," Raj said to him. "Lots of bodies are autopsied and there are smells and..."

"Don't worry," Bramble said, flying back to join the humans. "We know humans are uncomfortable to be around their dead, but we are different."

"Okay, don't say I didn't warn you," Raj said. "Just around this corner."

Bramble flitted ahead in a hurry to reach the morgue where they would find a clue and solve the case. A few hours had passed since they started, and he wanted to close the file and move on. Although, it was interesting to see how the body moved around. Did they autopsy Heath? He came to a stop as he saw who was waiting at the door to the autopsy room. Agnes.

"Were we expecting her?" Leith asked before Bramble could say anything.

Fernlight frowned and shook her head.

"Why are you here?" Bramble asked. "You should tell us when you will be here."

Agnes smiled at him and waited until the others arrived. "If you knew I was joining you, it would change how you use magic," she said. "Don't let me affect how you proceed. I am here to observe and advise if you want it."

Bramble slowed his wings until he was standing on the floor. He didn't like to hover over people when they talked. It was hard for him to read their emotions when they had to look up all the time.

"I'm happy to have you with us," Leith said. "Any advice you have is welcome."

Stupid sidhe. He shouldn't speak for them.

"I don't anticipate using magic here," Fernlight said. "Raj tells us humans find this autopsy procedure disturbing. Perhaps you would prefer to wait outside?"

"Is there a way for me to watch without being present?" Agnes seemed really curious.

"I don't know of a spell to let a human see from far away," Bramble said. "We could make one. Would that be a good use of magic?"

"Well, I think we will have to decide that when we see the spell in action. In the meantime, let's get on with this."

"It is very upsetting to be surprised," Bramble said. He hoped she would be kind and say she would stay outside the room if he was upset. She didn't.

"I hope you will become used to me popping in and out," she said. "Perhaps you'll find me useful at some point."

Bramble crossed his arms, ready to tell her to stay out.

"This is wasting time," Fernlight said before he could speak.

Agnes gestured to the door. "After you."

"You want some of this?" Raj asked, holding out a small pot of something medicinal-smelling.

"Thanks," Agnes said. She took some ointment and rubbed it on her upper lip.

"What is that?" Bramble asked. Were they using a magic potion?

"I told you it will smell bad," Raj said. "This covers up the odor enough to make the stink bearable."

Leith leaned in and wrinkled his nose. "These odors must be vile to make that a viable alternative. I prefer a charm to clean the air."

He took a handful of seeds from his pocket. "If you don't object, Agnes, I'm happy to share these."

"Perhaps next time," she said. "For now, we'll go with things we are sure will work."

Bramble refused the help, sure it was a sidhe trick. Fern-light took a seed but didn't activate the spell.

"Ready?" Agnes asked. No one told her to wait, so she opened the door.

Inside was a room that smelled clean at first, but Bramble detected an undertone of rot. He refused to ask for a seed from Leith.

CHAPTER FOURTEEN

Agnes waited for everyone to go through the door to the morgue. It wasn't the first time she'd witnessed an autopsy, but it didn't get easier with practice.

"Will you be okay with all the dead bodies?" Raj asked. "Some people have difficulty."

"No," she said. "I will focus on the magic and not on the presence of the dead."

"We will all be fine," Bramble said. "We have already seen this body."

Agnes saw Raj start to respond and didn't want to waste time with the argument. "Anyone who feels they can't handle it can leave and wait out here." She impatiently gestured for them to go ahead.

"No one is here," Bramble said. "And the body isn't on the table. We are in the wrong room."

"We'll need to wait for the medical examiner," Raj said. "They'll bring the body out when he gets here."

A banging sound came from the drawers where the bodies were kept. Agnes pushed down a wave of fear. She'd seen the body at the site. The noise wasn't a zombie fighting its way out to eat them. It was a victim just like the others.

"You should be done in a couple of days, right?" Raj asked. "I mean, you need to observe some of the magic and after that you can make your recommendations."

Not only the magical folk resented her presence. No investigator liked to be shadowed.

"Can we use magic when the body is brought out?" Bramble asked. "We can probably tell the medical examiner what happened, or why it's dancing."

"It's not that simple," she said. "First of all, the medical examiner will decide if you can participate. There are no guarantees he will agree."

"But if we can help," Fernlight said. "It seems that the humans always want to do things the hard way."

"I can assure you," Leith added, "we will not damage the body. We have some very subtle spells that can reveal a great deal of information."

She was looking forward to the time when magic could be done. Agnes had no desire to drag out her participation in the audit. She knew no matter what her recommendations were, her colleagues would challenge all magic use for as long as they could. Any defense lawyer who didn't fight the precedent was not doing the job right. She didn't tell the team about that, although Raj would know from his experience.

"First, remember the body belongs to the medical examiner right now. If he allows you to try some spells, you need to let me know exactly how you will cast them and what you expect to learn. I want this to work."

"And then you will go and write a report that says magic is good?" Bramble asked.

She smiled at his eagerness. It was hard to hold a grudge against a fairy. "My work will not be fast," she said. "I will need to see you do a wide range of spells. Or, if not witness them, I need learn about the spells."

"The druid might be your best choice for learning," Leith said. "The grove has an extensive library of magical lore."

Part of her itched to sit in the library and read accounts of spells, but that wasn't what she was here to do. "Perhaps later," she said, "but I expect to be with you and the others for the full duration of these two cases."

"Let's begin, shall we?" The medical examiner entered the room followed by an assistant. He pointed to a drawer and then the closest autopsy table. "This is an interesting one, and we have a large audience."

Agnes introduced everyone as the assistant did his best to gently transport the jerking body to the stainless steel table.

CHAPTER FIFTEEN

Lionel stood outside the minister's office. He'd expected something a little larger, and a little grander than this plain wooden door with a black plastic plaque on the wall bearing the minister's name and responsibility: *Connor Chan, Magical Affairs.*

"I guess we go in and start asking questions," he said to Rhodri, hoping the druid had a better idea.

"His staff should be eager to help," Rhodri said, "but we won't make any progress standing out here."

Lionel turned the handle and pushed the door open. Inside were two desks, one against a wall and the other facing them. Another door indicated a second office. One human woman sat behind the desk facing whoever came in. She was short and blond and thin and had a big smile that might have been sincere.

The other desktop was hidden under boxes of leaflets and scattered papers.

"You must be the detectives," the woman said. "I'm Minister Chan's aide, Ella Wade. Just call me Ella." She held out her hand and when neither responded, she asked, "Oh, don't you shake hands?"

Lionel blushed. "Of course, sorry." He took her hand and then stepped aside to give Rhodri access to her. He introduced himself and the druid.

"Great to meet you," Ella said. "Coffee? Tea?"

"I think we should start investigating," Lionel said. He looked around and found two chairs buried under more papers. He used a charm to pull the seats over and then waited for Ella to sit before he did. "We understand the minister has been missing for a day?"

"Well, there are obviously things I can't tell you," Ella said. "He attends confidential meetings that I only find out about after the fact. He's very committed to his portfolio. The country will be stronger when we are one people, he always says."

It didn't answer his question. Lionel tried a different approach. "If you can't tell us everything, we might not be able to find the minister. You know we can take an oath of confidentiality." He could tailor a secrecy spell to work for this circumstance.

"I thought you'd been briefed on the information. I don't have the authority to tell you." She looked worried and then her face cleared. "The secrets are probably nothing to do with the minister going missing. While you would think Magical Affairs would be controversial, there haven't been any threats or anything."

It would have been too easy if someone had sent a threatening note, or a ransom. But easy wouldn't be much of a lesson in investigation. "Did you contact the police?"

"No. I thought that if Queen Maeve could investigate, we could avoid publicity. It never looks good to have a minister disappear."

Rhodri leaned forward and said, "But the police should be told. I assume they are used to dealing with the politics."

"Should I contact them? Well, not the police, the RCMP, but I have no instructions…"

Was it normal to be instructed on what to do if your boss disappeared? As soon as the question hit his mind, Lionel realized that for a government minister, instructions for all kinds of scenarios would be on the books. He didn't want to upset Ella more than she already was. Her words had trailed off and now she was looking between him and Rhodri as if they had all the answers.

"We will take care of it," Rhodri said. "I'm sure Mamoru knows the protocols."

"Mamoru? Oh, Mr. Yamana. Yes, that's best." Ella relaxed at having that responsibility taken from her.

"Has this happened before?" Lionel asked. "Minister Chan going missing? Even for an hour?"

"No."

Lionel looked to Rhodri. If they didn't figure out how to get answers, this investigation was never going to start, let alone be solved.

Rhodri nodded to the papers all over the other desk. "Is it common for the records to be in such disarray? Perhaps there is a clue in it?"

Ella looked at the mess as though she'd just noticed it. "The volunteers left it like that," she said. "They are so helpful, but not good at keeping their area organized."

"We need a list of names of the volunteers," Rhodri said.

"But they wouldn't have kidnapped the minister. They're teenagers," Ella said, astonished at the idea of teenagers committing such a crime.

"But it is possible that a message might be hidden in the piles," Rhodri said, "and they might have seen or heard something that will help."

"I will get it for you, but please don't scare them off with hard questions. We need them."

Lionel wondered when Ella would realize that if they didn't solve the case, there would be a new minister and a new aide. He wouldn't bring it up, at least not until they had some reason to push her.

"And where else do you suggest we start?" Rhodri asked.

"The minister's calendar and contacts?" Ella said reluctantly. "I mean, not all the contacts, as some are quite confidential, but most of them."

Rhodri stood. "We'll start there, and we'll sort through the mess. Perhaps that will provide the next clue." He nodded toward the closed door. "Is that another office?"

"Yes, the minister's," Ella said. "I'll need to watch you while you're inside."

"Perfectly acceptable," Lionel said.

"Will you do magic?" Her voice was hopeful.

"If we need to," Lionel said. "We'll let you know before we cast anything." He wondered what Agnes would say about any spells they used.

CHAPTER SIXTEEN

When the body was set on the table, still moving, Bramble flew in to take a closer look.

"Move away until I tell you it's acceptable to approach," the medical examiner said. "This is my autopsy, and you are all guests."

Bramble lifted a little closer to the ceiling. The man didn't wear a name tag, so how was he supposed to know his name? "Mr. Examiner, we are here to help."

"You can call me Doctor Phillips," the man said. "I'm not convinced you will be doing anything helpful. This is unusual enough; I don't need to throw the rules out the door."

"But..." Bramble caught a look from Agnes that made him stop talking.

"Can we look first?" Raj said. "No one will touch anything. But before you cut, these guys might see something magical that explains the jerking."

Bramble was having a lot of trouble ignoring the body jumping and bouncing on the table. Only little movements, but constant and enough to make the dead man fall on the floor if no one paid attention. But Mr. Doctor Phillips was in charge and Bramble knew how he would feel if someone tried to tell him how to run his tribe, so he waited and let Raj clear the way.

"It's possible that the movement is not caused by magic," Raj said. "There are parasites, beetles, other unusual but mundane possibilities."

Leith took a half step toward the table. "Have you seen this before? The coloring or the twitching? After death?"

For the first time Bramble was hoping the sidhe would succeed. Anything that let them get closer would be good. Even if it was Leith.

"Not seen personally," Doctor Phillips said, "but I have not seen everything."

"Will waiting put your conclusions at risk?" Agnes asked. "I understand your concern, doctor, but I promise they will only look. You can record the whole thing and I am responsible for ensuring any magic used will comply with evidence rules."

The doctor looked around at everyone. Bramble let his wings take him to the ground. He couldn't see the body from so low, but he could hear the little bumps and ticks that the metal made from being banged around.

He kept his eyes on Leith to make sure the sidhe didn't do anything to make the doctor say no. When he said yes, Bramble would be the first to look, and Leith would be the last.

"Fine," Doctor Phillips said. "The camera is on. I suppose it's good for them to be involved from the start, if they need to be at all."

"Good," Bramble said and floated up to start looking.

"Wait," Fernlight said. "How does an autopsy work? It might be important."

Bramble was surprised when the doctor smiled. Was he

happy because he thought Fernlight would stop them looking?

"First, we do a visual inspection. Sometimes important information is just sitting on the skin. Next, we wash the body, collecting the water for testing. Then another visual, in case dirt was covering evidence. After all that is done, I cut them open, examine and measure the organs. I send samples for testing. I'll also look for signs of old injuries, or addiction."

"There are spells that will reveal the last for you," Fernlight said, "and possibly ones that could make the other steps easier."

"You can only look for now," Doctor Phillips reminded them.

"Perhaps I can offer a suggestion," Leith said. "What if we do our own visual examination and then discuss what magic can be used to reveal the cause of the movement, or any other clues?"

Raj turned to Agnes. "What exactly do we need to deal with to get magic approved?"

"I decide what you'll do to the body," Doctor Phillips reminded them.

Bramble felt like he was going to explode with impatience. Why did Leith have to say anything? They had permission. "Maybe I should look at the body while Leith slows everything down with suggestions."

Fernlight gave him that look again, but Bramble wasn't going to shut up.

Before he could say anything, Agnes spoke.

"Your team dynamics may do more to delay us than any discussion of magic."

Why did she say that? She was siding with the sidhe. He was just getting to like Agnes, and she turns out to be on the other side.

"Bramble, I need you to be patient," Fernlight said. "We will get a chance to look at the body, but we also need to talk about the magic."

Bramble looked at Doctor Phillips for help. Everyone was against him, but the doctor might be sensible. He was watching the body. "Fine," Bramble said. He'd wait until they were alone to talk to Fernlight about loyalty.

"So, we are agreed," Raj said. "We look and we can point out anything we think is important, but we don't touch. Okay, doctor?"

Bramble saw the doctor nod and didn't wait for any more discussion. He swooped down and looked closely at the body, being careful not to let the dead body touch him. The others crowded around, except Agnes and Raj. Humans wouldn't see anything important anyway.

The magical folk followed instructions not to interact with the body. Agnes had suggested the change from no touching to no interacting because she was sure at least one of them would take the opportunity to cast a spell. She would have if she had the ability.

Now they huddled with Raj, and Doctor Phillips was getting impatient.

"Did you find anything?" she asked, hoping to gain a little more time. As soon as the autopsy started, their chances to help would be gone.

Bramble floated out of the huddle; the others separated. He drifted toward the medical examiner, carefully avoiding the body.

"We didn't find any clues, but we came up with an idea for a spell." He landed to stand between Agnes and Doctor Phillips.

"I'm not happy with the idea of spells before I do my

work." Doctor Phillips crossed his arms over his chest. Agnes noticed the assistant become tightly focused on cleaning some equipment.

"The spell might not work when you cut him open," Bramble said. "Let me tell you what we will do, then you will understand."

All the usual annoyance at being stalled was gone from Bramble. Agnes figured some of the conversation in the huddle had been instructions on how to convince her and the medical examiner. Fairies seemed to learn fast; there was hope he'd stop sniping at the sidhe eventually.

"We will not disturb anything," Bramble said. "We will make the spell in a circle with the body, so we don't get any interference from the other dead people. We will use a smoke that will show us what happened when he was killed."

"The smoke will leave trace on the body," Doctor Phillips said.

His curiosity is overcoming his resistance, Agnes thought. He could have said no, but he'd left an opening to be persuaded.

"We will tell you the ingredients," Bramble said. He turned to look at Agnes. "She will need to know for her job. We need her permission too."

Agnes almost responded to say she was there to observe but realized that it would be a good thing if they thought she needed to approve the use of magic. Less likelihood of them sneaking in spells.

"It doesn't matter. I need to know what was on the body to start with. If a trace of something you use is already there, we'll miss it as evidence."

Bramble started to rise toward the ceiling. After a moment he realized what was happening and muttered something before landing on the floor again.

"This is very frustrating," he said. "You told us that you look at the body before you wash it, right?"

Doctor Phillips nodded.

"How do you store what you washed?"

"A plastic tub." He nodded to his assistant who held up a hose and gallon bucket. "Or more than one if the body is particularly dirty. This one is painted blue."

"This is not paint," Bramble said. "The skin is blue; it will not wash off."

"Okay, we'll see what happens."

Bramble looked at his team, but they had nothing to say. He looked at Agnes, who didn't help. He sighed. "Give me a minute to think, please."

He didn't wait for an answer, simply floated to within a foot of the ceiling and started circling the body.

"Are you okay with this nonsense?" Doctor Phillips asked, drawing Agnes' attention back to him.

"It's not nonsense," she said. "I don't know enough about it to say either way. But this team solved two very complicated cases. And they've used magic to some extent."

"What do you think? Should I let them do this spell?"

"Your choice, but yes, like you, I would make sure it didn't interfere with the usual process. I would be interested to see what they find once that was clear."

She meant what she said, but it didn't fit well with her assignment. She was starting to sound like an advocate for the magical folk. Not a good path to take if she was meant to be neutral.

Bramble returned. "What if we wait until you've looked at the body and washed it? Then we can put the bucket inside the circle in case something that washed off is important."

"How do you break a circle?" Doctor Phillips asked. "If something goes wrong, how do we get out?"

"From the outside you would just make a space in the salt

we use to make the circle." Bramble cocked his head at the medical examiner. "It would not be a good idea to do that. If something is going wrong in the circle, it could escape. You should let us decide how to solve any problems."

Doctor Phillips stepped toward the body, looked at the investigators, at his assistant, and finally at Agnes. "We'll do it. I will be inside with you so I can make sure you don't interfere with my job."

"Yes!" Bramble floated to Fernlight. "We can do it."

Fernlight smiled. "Thank you, Agnes. I think you helped."

"It's the last time I'll do that," she said. "I'm not here to help or hinder."

CHAPTER SEVENTEEN

Bramble watched closely as Doctor Phillips did his job. The man looked really close at the body; sometimes he had to dodge when a jerk made it bounce. Then he asked his assistant to wash the dead man. Bramble expected soap and water, but only water flowed gently from the spout. How would anything wash off without magic or soap?

The water ran clear, mostly. A little regular dirt went in the bucket. But the skin was still blue when they finished.

Doctor Phillips stepped back from the table and looked at Fernlight. "I'm ready for you to do your magic."

Suddenly there was a lot of action. Raj and Agnes stood where Fernlight told them to. The sidhe and Fernlight set a double circle of salt to protect the rest of the world from the magic. Bramble hovered near the body and tried to anticipate the next bounce. It was always twitching, but every once in a while, the body jerked hard enough to leave the table and drop back.

Fernlight started to explain, drawing his attention to her. "We are going to cast a charm. There's no smoke or anything that will get into the evidence. It should show us what happened to the person in the moments before he died."

"Will we be able to see the result?" Raj asked. "It would be helpful. I mean, you will know what the magic does, but we might notice something you don't."

"Yes," Bramble said. "Like a movie on the Internet. You'll see the same as us. Do you have any other questions? When we start, you shouldn't interrupt us. Leith and I will do the magic. Fernlight will be ready to protect you if we wake something."

He looked carefully at everyone. The doctor and Agnes would be in the circle, but the assistant would not. His job was to make sure no one came into the room. Bramble suspected that Doctor Phillips expected more from his assistant than that. But when Bramble argued that everyone should be inside, Doctor Phillips said he would stop them doing the spell if he insisted.

He looked at the assistant with a stern expression. "You will not break the circle. It will be very bad if you try to end the spell."

"Yes. I heard you the first three times. I promise to stay by the door. Will I see anything?"

"No. The protection will look misty to you."

Bramble was both eager to do this spell and find their answers, and fearful that Leith would do something to undermine him. He could only hope Fernlight would make sure the sidhe stayed under control.

"The circle will encompass the examination table," Leith said. "We need to make a circle, not a rectangle. Spirits find corners handy for hiding. I'll make it as small as possible so that we don't have any bleed of information from the other bodies in the room. Please try to stand still while we work."

Bramble observed as Leith created the protective circle. He was making it with only a little salt. The line almost as thin as Heath's salt strings, Bramble saw a curly pattern, but only a few grains wide. He felt power rise as the circle closed them off from the room.

"Let's not delay," Leith said. He stood to one side of the table and waited.

Bramble flitted to face him. With so many in the small circle, the heat rose and soon everyone was going to be uncomfortable. "Is everyone ready?"

Leith didn't wait for answers. He tossed the end of a fine silver chain to Bramble. The spell shimmered between them. Bramble rose to create a fine screen of shimmering magic.

"Show us the event," Leith said.

Bramble cocked his head to catch the action. Night, two people walked in the shadows of the room; the man who ended up on the table below him and a shadowy figure wearing a hooded jacket.

They were talking, but the spell didn't show sounds. The hooded man raised his hand and the body on the table jerked. The picture of the live man didn't move. The images weren't clear. They kept fuzzing out.

The movie showed the hooded man raising a curved knife. Then the vision blinked, and the dead man lay on the floor. The hooded man pulled out a length of rope. He raised his hand and the dead man rose from the floor, twitching. The images fuzzed again and when it cleared, the corpse was hanging from the ceiling and the hooded one walking out of the scene.

The real body on the table jerked all the time now. Like he was watching too and wanted to escape.

They waited but nothing else happened, and after a few minutes, the images faded. Bramble floated across to hand Leith both ends of the chain. Fernlight broke the circle and cool air washed over Bramble.

"He knew we could do this," Raj said. "He acted like there was a camera and he avoided looking up."

"Yes," Leith said. "Even with the interference, I saw that."

"What was getting in your way?" Doctor Phillips asked. "I mean, I'm impressed, and I plan to recommend we use this process, but only if you can clear the result up."

Bramble looked around the room. There was no magic here. "Maybe all the other bodies got in the way? You can try the spell in a separate room. Or maybe part of the spell that killed this man hid the details."

It wasn't helpful, but his job was to solve the murder, not to help the humans with their stupid processes.

"We know the killer was a man, right?" Raj said. "I mean, not a fairy or some other kind of magical person who looks so different."

Bramble didn't want to tell him the truth because it only made things complicated. But Raj was part of his team. "Or the interference might be because of a glamor. The spell didn't help."

"It did," Doctor Phillips said. "Whoever did this, they used magic."

CHAPTER EIGHTEEN

Lionel looked at the office from the doorway. Rhodri and the aide were already at the desk, but he wanted to see the room before they searched for anything.

The desk was old; a slab of oak and two columns of drawers for legs. The chair was black leather and well worn. Bookshelves lined the left and right walls, a couple of chairs sat beside a small glass table. He tried to picture Maeve sitting in this office drinking tea and talking about the future. Not a chance. She would have required him to come to the court.

On the desk, an open laptop shared space with a coaster holding a coffee cup, with stale coffee inside if he identified the smell right. Papers and bound reports piled on the desk, on the floor, and on the bookshelves. Pretty clearly a real working office. This minister was busy and didn't worry about making things look tidy.

"His appointments are on the computer," Ella said. "How far back do you want?"

"Can we access the information through searches? And take a printout with us?" Lionel was sure they wouldn't be able to take a politician's computer away. Especially since Ella insisted on watching while they conducted the search.

"I should be able to order you a printout of everything in the last two months," Ella said. "It would be easier if you could just search here. You'll need to read the printouts through, no search feature."

Lionel wondered if she was really being helpful, or if she had something to hide. Something they wouldn't think to search for but would discover in reading the hard copy.

"We can use spells to search printed documents," Rhodri said, "and we don't want to keep bothering you to access the computer. Unless we can take that?"

Ella almost said yes. Lionel saw her open her lips to speak and then close them with a suspicious look in her eyes. "No. I would have to ask for authorization. We don't want any official eyes on this yet."

She thought Rhodri had cast a spell to compel her, but no magic had been done. Her stare fixed on Rhodri, looking for evidence of the glow. Lionel smiled. Humans didn't know that the glow didn't come if you used a pre-spelled charm.

"You don't need authorization to request the printout?" Lionel joined Rhodri at the desk. The computer screen was blank.

"I request them all the time. Mostly only a week's worth of appointments so the minister can complete his paperwork. No one will question a full printout."

"Do you know the password?" Rhodri asked.

Ella leaned in and pressed a key. The screen lit up with the calendar open. "He doesn't remember to lock it."

She stepped back to let them access the device, but stood close to the windows so she could watch every action they took.

Lionel sat in the chair and started reviewing the appointments. "How long will it take to get the printout?" No meeting with Maeve? Surely, they weren't meeting in secret.

She stiffened. "Only ten or so minutes. But I am not leaving you here alone."

"If we had both," Rhodri said, "it might speed up our investigation. It is difficult for me to help when we are crowded around the small screen."

She thought his request over and then made them follow her to the reception area. She typed a few lines in an email. "It will print in the minister's office."

Lionel and Rhodri followed her back to the laptop and started searching again. Ella standing over them, suspicious of their every move, made concentrating hard, but he tried to ignore her.

"There's nothing here with Maeve," he said to Rhodri. "There should be something."

"He met with her a week ago at the court," Ella said. "If I remember correctly, Tuesday at noon. He was gone for the rest of the day."

Lionel flipped the screen back to the date. "Nothing."

Ella stepped forward. "But it was recorded. I checked. Why would it be gone?"

The printer started pushing out pages of information. "Did he use a code name?" Lionel couldn't think why the minister would want secrecy. He was responsible for magical affairs, so he would be expected to meet with magical folk.

"No. Can I look?" Ella gestured toward the keyboard. "Maybe I can find something."

Lionel wanted to say no, but if Ella wanted to change the records, she could have done so anytime. The printer finished, so he stepped back and watched Ella while Rhodri grabbed the pages.

Ella looked back several weeks, then typed in a few searches. "It's all gone." She stared at the screen as if it would suddenly change. "None of her appointments are here. No contact information. We provided a phone just for ministry business."

Rhodri put the papers on the desk. "Were these printed from the information on the computer?"

"You mean would they be different? It depends. If someone erased the information today, the paper copies should have the missing information because the data comes from a backup."

Lionel flipped through pages until he reached the day when the minister met Maeve. "Nothing."

"We will need to search the office," Rhodri said.

"Can't you do magic to bring back the information?" Ella sounded desperate.

"We have never succeeded in that," Rhodri answered. "When digital information is removed, it is replaced with something. We cannot go beyond that act."

Lionel remembered how Kali had removed information about herself from the Internet in the first days after the prophecy. Someone had been able to find that again. But it wasn't time to delve into that. If the druids haven't found a way to bring back deleted files, it probably can't be done.

CHAPTER NINETEEN

Bramble stared at the body on the table. He knew so many spells he could do to find out what went wrong before. Even if they couldn't see the person who killed him, they might find magic residue or maybe learn who committed the crime.

"I have other spells," he said. "We can help more."

Doctor Phillips moved closer to the table and made his assistant stand on the other side. "I need to finish my work before you do anything else."

The body jerked so hard it lifted off the table and then banged back down.

The assistant stepped back and shook his head when Doctor Phillips motioned him closer. "Don't be a fool, Milo. There's nothing alive here. You'll be safe."

"How can you be sure? We've never had anything to do with magic before. This body should be coming out of rigor, but it's still jerking. Maybe we'll end up the same way." The assistant took another step back.

"Zombies don't exist," Doctor Phillips said. "At least, we've never encountered one. Do magical zombies exist somewhere?"

He'd looked at Leith when he asked, but Bramble zoomed closer to answer. "When things are dead, they stay dead. If you let us do magic, we can figure out why this one is not doing that."

"And if I let you cast spells, you might destroy any evidence. I'm not having this discussion again. I let you do one spell, and now you need to leave the body to me."

He's mad at us for no reason!

Bramble didn't care. An angry human frightened him no more or less than a happy one. If they waited for Doctor Phillips to cut open the body, the magic might dissipate.

"Perhaps I can offer a suggestion," Leith said. "If my colleagues agree, and Ms. Swiftwing has no objection, I think I have a charm that will calm the body."

The stupid sidhe was going to make Doctor Phillips even madder, and he would send them out. Bramble wanted to observe the autopsy. There might be a clue inside the body, or he might notice something that will solve the case.

"What exactly do you propose?" Doctor Phillips asked.

"I think your assistant would be happier if the body doesn't jump up to meet you during the process?"

"Yeah," Milo said. "I'm still not happy about the magic, but this jerking is way too weird."

"How were you going to deal with the movement?" Leith asked.

Why is everyone just watching and not stopping the sidhe?

"I thought if I cut the tendons at the joints, I would remove the mechanical ability for the body to move, but that's a lot of cutting."

Doctor Phillips pointed at the big joints, but the fingers were moving too. That meant he would need to cut all the joints. "Doing that would take a long time," Bramble said.

"And it might have an effect on the results. We don't

know how long the body will hold off on rigor or if the magic will speed up decomposition," Doctor Phillips said. "No matter what we do, it will change the findings. What do you suggest?"

Leith stepped forward to the body before looking around at everyone. "I think a variation on a stasis spell might help. What do you think?"

Fernlight shrugged. "It's worth a try," she said. "The spell simply slows everything down. I mean, the person is dead and still moving, so we can't be sure."

"So, the body would still move, but so slowly we can continue the autopsy?" Doctor Phillips asked. "I can't imagine that causing problems in my report. Agnes?"

"If you are comfortable with using stasis magic, I have no argument."

"But what about your worry that any magic would be wrong?" Bramble asked. "Doctor Phillips, you said no magic!"

The doctor looked from Bramble to the body and back. "I know I said that," he finally answered. "The problem is that magic is already interfering. I'm not aware of anything mundane that can cause this. No insect or parasite would still be this active. Your man's suggestion seems the least intrusive."

Why did Leith get to do magic? It was unfair, and Bramble got ready to say so until he looked at Fernlight for an ally. She gave him the look. She thought he was being petty. That he just objected because Leith suggested it. He didn't trust the sidhe, and she was probably right. So, he pressed his lips together and nodded. The spell might fail anyway.

Leith pulled a small stone from his pocket. "Fernlight, or Bramble, can you modify this spell to allow the doctor to do his work through the barrier?"

Bramble flew down to look closely at the stone. It carried a strong stasis spell to stop all time around the body, but no one would be able to reach through.

He looked at Fernlight. "Can you weaken it?"

She shook her head. "The magic is too different."

Well, as usual, a fairy has to fix a sidhe problem. Fine! "Hold the charm steady," Bramble said firmly to Leith. "I will make the effect much weaker. Do not try any tricks."

Leith smiled like he didn't think Bramble was smart enough. "I had no intention of doing anything."

Bramble gathered his thoughts. The sidhe magic looked plainer than fairy magic. Not pretty, but very efficient. He needed to drain the magic to something. He looked around. Nothing he could use came to mind because everything was dead. Metal, wood, plastic. He needed something living. It wouldn't cause too much problem, and Leith would release the spell right away.

"Come here, Raj," Bramble said. "This won't hurt at all."

He placed one hand on Raj and the other on the stone. The magic moved quickly, turning Raj rigid in seconds.

"Done. The spell will only slow things down a little." Bramble floated up to the ceiling to watch the action.

"What did you do to him?" Doctor Phillips asked, pointing to Raj.

"Oh, Leith will free him, but I had to put the extra power somewhere."

Fernlight stepped up to hold Raj steady while Leith placed the stone in the body's right hand. "When you need to work on that, I'll move the charm. If you touch the stone, it will place you in stasis."

The body stopped moving. Bramble floated down to look carefully. He saw the tiny movements that would build to a jerk, but the spell did make it seem like nothing moved.

"Bramble, a little warning next time," Raj said as Leith released him.

"I didn't hurt you," Bramble said, keeping his eyes on the autopsy table.

CHAPTER TWENTY

The autopsy was interesting and also awful. Bramble floated as close as possible without getting in the way. The rest of the team stood in the corner watching a screen that showed them everything. They didn't get to hear the squelchy noises or the loud cracks of bones breaking over there. Well, not as loud as Bramble heard them.

"The victim is in his mid to late thirties. He shows signs of substance abuse but is otherwise healthy," Doctor Phillips told the autopsy story to a recorder.

Bramble kept a careful eye on the whole body to see if it would start jerking again, but nothing moved.

"The Y-incision reveals healthy lung tissue. Observation of the organs reveals no obvious chronic damage."

"Why do you say that?" Bramble asked. "Are you surprised?"

The assistant looked up and frowned at Bramble. "Don't interrupt Doctor Phillips during the exam."

"But the answer might help." Bramble hoped he would find the important clue. That's why he was enduring this cutting and snapping of bones. "You don't know if magic can explain anything."

"Yes, Bramble, I am surprised," Doctor Phillips said. He pointed to some bruises and what might be bug bites on the arms. "Outside, he looks like a junkie. Someone who is addicted to drugs. See these marks? Needles make similar ones."

"Why are you surprised now?" Bramble forced his wings to drop him closer to the body. *He won't grab you!*

"From the outside, a junkie, but on the inside, a healthy man. Things like that help to solve cases."

The assistant handed Doctor Phillips a new knife. "You want to take the organs now?"

Doctor Phillips nodded. "We'll weigh the organs and take samples for testing. Maybe he only recently started abusing drugs. Maybe someone made it look like he was an addict."

"This is very interesting," Bramble said. "I don't think magic could have preserved his insides, but maybe someone used his outsides for spells."

"I didn't think magical folk did bad magic," the assistant said. "Or is that image control to make us mere humans feel safe?"

"Milo, I don't want that kind of talk here. We don't take sides or bring politics into the room." Doctor Phillips took the knife.

Bramble floated a little higher just in case something spurted out. "We don't. We don't murder people either. Humans do, and humans try to do magic all the time."

"Bramble," Fernlight called from the safety of the corner, "we shouldn't make assumptions."

She said it like he was the only one who didn't trust humans, but he wasn't. They all had reason to be wary. Fernlight in particular. She saw how humans tried to use magic for all kinds of awful things in the last two cases.

"What's this?" Doctor Phillips asked. "Could it be magic?"

Bramble spun around. The doctor held up a clamp containing something coated in red and purple mush. He floated in closer. The thing was a tiny carving of a beetle, the mush was part of the dead man.

CHAPTER TWENTY-ONE

"A charm." Leith leaned in and sniffed. "I don't recognize the magic. But, I would wager a seat at Maeve's next feast that this is the cause of the motions. Perhaps much more."

Milo held out a metal pan. Doctor Phillips dropped the charm in and stepped back. "Is it still active?" the doctor asked. "Do we need to take precautions?"

Bramble hovered over the pan. "It is weakening already. Nothing to be worried about. This is wizard magic, I think. Not normal though, and I can't tell who the wizard is."

"I'll order tests to find out if there are any toxins," Doctor Phillips said.

Fernlight moved around Leith to look in the pan. "We should test the magic first, before it fades completely."

"Any tests you do may invalidate mine." Doctor Phillips moved the pan away. "You can test after we finish the normal checks."

"And how long will that take?" Fernlight asked. "We have only an hour or so before the magic is gone. And that's only if it doesn't fade faster now that the charm is out of the body."

"I don't know if I should..." Doctor Phillips said.

"I'll call Mamoru," Raj said. "No one knows what to do. We need him to decide."

"Is that what you do?" Agnes asked. "Ask for permission?"

"This is the first time," Bramble said.

"I meant, for me and my report. If you needed to ask for permission before, it will help me to know that."

Fernlight watched Raj as he talked. "No. We don't ask permission. But as Bramble said, we haven't been in this situation before."

"And you can't always wait for permission," Agnes said. "Don't worry; I won't suggest that. It makes no sense."

"Mamoru agrees that the magic is more important. He'll send you the authorization in a minute," Raj said. "Can I suggest a compromise? How about you take some scrapings to test, and then my team checks the magic?"

Doctor Phillips thought about it for what felt like ages. Bramble could feel the magic fading.

"Milo, take samples of the body matter and a small scrape of the wood."

"Let me do the wood scrape," Bramble said. He floated a bit closer to Milo as the man put on a second pair of gloves and took a small instrument from the row laid out on a cloth.

"Stay back until I'm done." Milo didn't look up.

"Let the fairy take the sample," Doctor Phillips said. "Fernlight, can you tell if the body still needs to be under the calming spell?"

Milo finished and took a big step back. Bramble chose a delicate knife to take a slice of wood.

"Leith can check. But what if there are more charms?"

"Where do I put this?" Bramble asked.

Milo pointed to a row of vials. "In one of those."

"I suppose we can't take the risk now that the victim is opened up. A jerk now would cause evidence to hit the floor," Doctor Phillips said. "It's feeling crowded in here. I need one of the magical folk, but the rest of you must leave."

Bramble picked up the pan with the amulet and flitted back to join the others in the corner. He was not going to stay here alone with three humans — even if one of them was dead.

"I'll stay," Fernlight said. "Perhaps the team could use an office or a lab close by, in case we run into trouble?"

Doctor Phillips called for someone to find them a place to do their own tests.

This room is as bad as the autopsy one, Bramble thought. The same drawers lined the wall—the same smell of dead bodies covered with some cleaning solutions. But there were no bodies in the drawers and no humans to argue with. Maybe it would work.

"Put the things on the floor," Bramble said. "We need a circle."

Leith took a parcel from his pocket and poured lavender salt in a circle, leaving a gap so they could get inside when they were ready. Bramble flew along the line, checking for breaks. The salt was pretty, but it was important to make sure the sidhe hadn't made any mistakes.

"Okay. Who is coming in?" Bramble looked at the two humans, hoping neither would be willing.

"Agnes, did you want to join us?" Leith asked. He gave Bramble a stare when he buzzed in to say not to let a human in.

"No, I will wait outside," Agnes said. "I'll join you in a circle later. Raj?"

"Maybe later, too," he said. "We might be the problem. It's worth letting the magical folk do their thing alone for now."

The humans were smarter than Bramble expected.

Now it's only me and the stupid sidhe!

"Fine," Bramble said, "I'll make the protection clear so you can see what is happening."

He buzzed into the center and hovered over the items. When Leith closed the circle, Bramble said the words to allow the others to observe and then pulled out a handful of fairy chalk.

"I know of spells that don't leave residue," Leith said.

"I can call the chalk back." Did he think fairies just left their magic lying around?

"Then we should start," Leith said. He sat on the floor tiles and waited.

Bramble said the words to activate the magic quietly because Leith would try to steal the spell if he wasn't careful.

A fine cloud of powder drifted down. When it got to the items on the floor, Bramble expected to see the last scene of the dead man played out, but nothing happened. He flew down close and whispered the spell again. He saw a ripple in the powder, but it didn't show anything.

He called the chalk back to his hand. "Try your magic," he said, trying not to sound worried.

Leith sent sparkling magic to the center of the circle. Nothing happened.

"It seems we're going to have to work harder to get our information," Leith said.

Bramble told him to clear the circle, and when it was done, he said, "I don't think our magic works in these surroundings. We can try again at the office."

CHAPTER TWENTY-TWO

"Does he keep anything personal here?" Lionel asked as they looked through the tenth pile of papers in the minister's office.

Ella frowned and looked around the room. "Not really. Some ministers like to decorate the office with memorabilia or family items. But Minister Chan keeps his office and his home separate."

Lionel didn't look forward to talking to the family and asking for an item they might cherish, better an item from the office. The more the person cared about the item, the stronger the spell. "The item doesn't need to be big."

Rhodri ran his finger along the edges of another pile. "You are thinking a tracking spell?"

"It could be that easy," Lionel said. He stared at a flyer for a town hall meeting, whatever that was.

"You don't think Maeve would have already done one?"

"She's never been here," Lionel said. Then, thinking about what he'd said, he turned back to Ella who was sitting at her desk watching carefully over the rim of her tea mug. "Have any sidhe been here? Anyone who might be magical?"

"Not that I can remember," Ella said. "The office isn't exactly set up for visitors."

No, it seems to be set up as a storeroom. And from everything Ella said, nothing about the room is normal for a politician's office.

"Is there a reason the minister has this kind of location?" Rhodri asked.

He was looking at Lionel. Perhaps they were both thinking the same thing. The government didn't think magical affairs was an important topic.

"He's new, and his portfolio is new. So, no one knows what kind of traffic he'll get. We're on the short list for a bigger space, but that can mean years."

"What does he do, exactly?" Lionel said. "What is a town hall?"

Ella stood and joined them at the table. "He mostly meets with community groups. He wants to meet with magical folk, but Maeve is the only one who has been willing. The town hall is a meeting where people ask questions. We learn what's in the voter's mind."

"People, or humans?" Rhodri asked. "Do you distribute these invitations to anyone with questions?"

Ella picked up a sheet from the pile. "How would we? We post these in coffee shops, and we drop them door-to-door. But how do we invite fairies and other magical folk?"

Lionel knew the answer, but would any magical people be welcome? Would they be safe?

"The best way would be to provide the druids with a supply. We can reach out to the rest of the community without giving away magical secrets."

"That building in the tree circle?" Ella asked. "People get lost all the time trying to pass through the forest."

"On purpose," Rhodri said. "We all feel safer when we are hard to find on a whim." He took a small ring from his pocket. "Put this on a chain and hang it around your neck, and the trees will admit you. I'll inform the archdruid today. Do not share the ring with anyone."

Ella's eyes were wide as she accepted the ring. It was too small for her fingers, but she wore a thin gold chain. Lionel helped her with the clasp and then stepped back.

"Can I go anywhere magical with this?" She took a canvas bag from a drawer and started dropping flyers inside. "Like the sidhe court?"

"You will need an invitation from Maeve," Lionel said. "Rhodri can only give you access to the grove."

She patted her blouse where the ring hung. "I'll be careful."

Lionel figured Trahaearn would send a druid to the meeting to test if it was safe. "What about a personal diary?" Maybe Ella hadn't thought a book would be useful.

"No. Everything was online." She took a key from a tray on her desk. "If he wanted to keep something private, he'd lock it in a drawer."

Interesting that he would want to secure a personal item but let his assistant have a key.

They returned to the inner office and stood behind the desk. Ella unlocked the four desk drawers. "Please don't disturb anything."

The first drawer contained a supply of pens and scratch pads. The second a bag of candy and a handful of old maps of Vancouver. The third, letters and a string of red beads. The fourth held a mirror.

"Are the beads his?" Lionel asked. He could sense power emanating from them.

"Oh, yes. A Feng Shui thing. The mirror too. I don't completely understand the theory, but it's a way to keep good spirits in and bad spirits out."

"I know what Feng Shui is," Rhodri said. "It isn't magic but does have some effect. We need to take a bead."

"But he'll notice when he gets back. And the protection might stop working. If it is, I guess. I mean, he did disappear."

Lionel touched the string. "He's handled this enough to make it worth using."

"How about we use a charm to replace the whole string of beads?" Rhodri asked. "Not a good luck charm, but a protective one."

Ella considered the idea. "What will happen to the beads?"

"We can return them undamaged," Lionel said. *Will she believe us? I should be more positive.* "I promise we can put them back without any sign they were used to track the minister. He won't be upset if we find him."

"Can't you do the spell here?" Ella asked. "That way, you don't need to take the beads anywhere."

"We need more room to cast the spell," Rhodri said.

There is plenty of room. We don't need more than a space to mix the ingredients.

"Can I come too?" Ella asked.

She wants to see us do the spell. Her reluctance is not about the beads at all. Lionel kicked himself for not seeing her fascination earlier.

"I'm afraid we can't allow you to join us this time," Rhodri said. "We must show the proof to a woman who monitors our magic use. She would not allow you to attend."

Why didn't I think of that? Agnes wouldn't care, but Ella doesn't know that.

CHAPTER TWENTY-THREE

Ella took a deep breath. "No. The police will need to have everything in place when they investigate."

Lionel wondered how humans got anything done. Going back to Maeve to tell her they allowed this little human to stop them wouldn't placate her. He looked at Rhodri for help with no success. They couldn't even talk ideas through with Ella standing guard.

"When are the police arriving?" he asked.

"I didn't call them yet." Ella closed the drawer. "And it will be the RCMP because the minister is a politician."

"So," Rhodri said, "you aren't going to start an official investigation, and you won't let us move forward on the current path."

"It sounds bad when you put it like that." She sat, looking tinier in the minister's chair. "I want him found, but this magic thing is confusing."

Lionel moved away from the desk hoping she would relax if the drawer was out of his reach. He could cast a spell, but they needed Ella's trust. And this was one of the ways to integrate human and magical worlds. Undermining that effort was bound to cause problems.

"Why are you working in the magical affairs office if you don't trust magic?" Rhodri asked.

The druid was having a much easier time dealing with the objections. Lionel knew he could solve problems, but thinking around a problem was a skill he hadn't yet acquired.

"Admin assigned me. And Minister Chan is a good boss." She crossed her arms and stiffened her back. "Why?"

"I wondered how you managed to work every day with something you clearly don't trust." Rhodri's voice was calm and projected kindness.

Ella relaxed a little. "I need to learn more before I trust anything. I will take the flyers to your grove, but until magical people participate in the process... Well, I guess I don't think they care about it if they won't get involved."

They think we don't care. It's about survival for us.

"We can't wait," Lionel said. "We are all leery of what will happen, and, in the past, any time magical folk involved themselves in human affairs, people died. Not humans either, the weight of death always fell on our folk."

"We don't know if things have changed," Ella said. "We don't know what you've set in motion that could kill us, or even did in the past."

Now they'd found the real problem. Ella believed the rumors that magical folk were responsible for plagues and wars.

"Perhaps we need a break," Rhodri said.

Ella jumped up from the desk. "Yes. I need the restroom. You can wait in the hall."

She didn't even trust them in the public part of the office. Lionel tried to remember when the situation turned bad. She was friendly earlier. The discussion about the town hall was pleasant. As soon as they found the string of beads, barriers slammed between the human and magical folk.

Ella offered to point out the public restrooms, but Rhodri said they would wait for her. She hurried down the corridor, looking to make sure they hadn't moved before turning left.

"We should simply take it and leave a glamor that the beads are still there," Rhodri said. "We can replace them as soon as we've done the spells."

It was tempting. "No. There's something wrong with them. Did you notice the effect?"

"That's when we started arguing?" He nodded. "You think it happened because someone interfered? Or maybe bad work on the Feng Shui?"

"A spell will tell us. We'll go back in and ask her to open the drawers again. I'll distract her and you take one bead."

Ella returned as Rhodri agreed. Lionel hoped he didn't trigger some defense charm by taking a bead. The disruption spell, whatever the cause, was getting in the way. And taking it back to the office might reinforce the distrust building as the team grew.

Ella seemed friendly again, so it didn't take much to convince her to reopen the drawers. Lionel engaged her in a search of the pens and pads in the drawer while Rhodri used magic to release one bead from the string. The disruption spell snapped as he untied the string to release a bead, lifting some of the pressure to bully or trick Ella into complying with their requests. Their search was coming to an end and there was no time to create a glamor to hide the fact that a bead was missing.

"I think the best action is to talk to the family," Rhodri said. "We will find something in his home and use that to track him."

Lionel stepped back from his search. Ella smiled at them

and didn't seem affected this time. "Please be gentle with his family," she said. "They are very worried."

Back outside, Lionel said, "His family can't be that concerned. They haven't gone public."

"Yes. That is interesting." Rhodri turned toward the office. "We're going to try the tracking spell first, right?"

"Yes, and we'll see what we can find out about that disruption spell."

Outside the minister's building, Lionel looked at the string of beads. "Why didn't you just take one?"

Rhodri dropped it into his pocket. "A glamor is more stable if we don't have to make it blend with the whole thing. And I sense something wrong with it. I wanted to analyze what kind of protection this Feng Shui gives."

Lionel pulled out his phone. "We can research that right now," he said. "Look, there are all kinds of articles online."

"We need to test the string as well as see what it's supposed to do." Rhodri patted his pocket. "If the charm is for protection, why has he disappeared?"

Lionel looked around to find a place to do the tracking spell. No convenient landscaping or private nooks. "Do you remember if we're near a park or something that we can use to do a discrete tracking spell?"

Rhodri looked at him. "We need Agnes's permission. We should go back to the office. Everything we need is there."

"But what if Mamoru decides we can't use a stolen item?" Lionel wanted this case to be over. The fastest way to do that was to follow the minister's movements to his current location. When they found him, he would be free to start digging into Heath's murder, or maybe the recent case. Something Maeve couldn't control.

"We didn't steal it. We borrowed it. I fully intend to return it to the desk when we are done."

And if we can't, we are no longer borrowing anything.

"We can find the spell ingredients anywhere," Lionel said. "Going back to the office will complicate things."

"We need to check with Agnes," Rhodri said.

"We've done tracking spells before," Lionel said. "We should be able to get away with one more."

"A dark path to go down, Lionel. By saying 'get away with,' you imply we are doing something wrong. I'm not willing to risk losing the case over your impatience."

Not impatience. But the thought didn't ring true. It wasn't like him to bend the rules. Just because Maeve asked them, no, ordered them, to find the minister, didn't mean she could run the investigation.

"Lionel? We should go back to the office. We need to do this right, so we aren't under scrutiny all the time. This is exactly what Mamoru wanted to avoid."

The office did have all the ingredients and a space dedicated to spell casting. And help. The brownies, Bramble's children, Kim. Everyone could help.

"We need to do this right away," Lionel said. "When we return, grab the ingredients, and we'll follow up on the leads."

"I can let Mamoru and Agnes know what we are planning," Rhodri said, "while we walk."

And have them say no? "When we get back," Lionel said, "I guess before we do the spell. I just hope nothing happens to the minister while we delay."

CHAPTER TWENTY-FOUR

Back at the office, they were waiting for Lionel and Rhodri to arrive. Bramble wanted to keep working, but even he had to agree there wasn't anything to do until they could try some spells on the charm. And Mamoru wanted them all to give reports. And probably he was talking for Maeve too. She would want to know what was going on with the missing minister case.

When Rhodri called, he said he had something new in the case for Maeve. Maybe that would be enough to report.

"There is nothing to tell you," Bramble said to Mamoru. "We went to the autopsy. We have the charm, and we need to do some magic on it. Why do we all need to be together?"

Mamoru didn't look up from the box containing the charm from the dead man. "It is useful for everyone to hear what is going on with the investigations. Sometimes insights come from reporting."

Agnes was sitting with Kim going over some of the magic Kim had experienced. Why did she want a human to tell her about magic? Leith stood and excused himself to go stand in a corner, probably to help him spy for Maeve. The brownies were still lurking under a desk. Briar and Thistle buzzed around everyone's heads. Too much was going on with no progress.

"Did you feel anything from the magical paths?" Agnes asked Kim. "Do you think it affected you in some permanent way?"

"No. Other than being a bit claustrophobic in the tunnel, I felt like me." Kim made a note on the list of spells she'd seen or been part of. "Tracking spells are your first priority. Then anything that can reveal something about the crime. At some point after that, restraining spells need to be assessed."

"Maeve is present," Leith said like he was announcing her entrance. "I allowed her to expand her communication circle so she can hear what we say and can ask questions."

Stupid sidhe always making themselves important!

"I suppose communication spells need to be on the list, too," Agnes said. "I'm going to be busy."

"We don't communicate with magic when we are investigating," Bramble said. "We use phones if we need to talk to someone who isn't with us."

Agnes glanced at the list again and then back to Bramble. "I will still need to understand the impact. Perhaps it will help us in other ways. I wonder if witnesses can testify through magical communicating?"

Just when he got mad at her, Agnes said something he liked. Her suggestion reminded him of what Heath was doing: trying to make magic useful to humans and easier to do. "Not until we get approval of the spells we need."

Agnes nodded.

Lionel and Rhodri stepped through the secret door to the back office.

"Good, now we can do the report and get on with our important work," Bramble said.

"Keeping your client updated is important, fairy." Maeve's

voice came from behind Leith. "If I do not hear from you frequently, I will make sure you are not hiding things from me."

Leith will spy for you; don't pretend you won't get reports from him.

"Not as important as solving the case," Bramble said. Then he shut up because everyone was looking at him with stern faces. Even his own children.

Mamoru stood and drew their attention to the whiteboards at the back of the room. "You usually put your progress and ideas here," he said. "And you generally have clues and ideas hidden from me. Please continue with that process, but do not hide things from Ms. Swiftwing."

"You knew?" Bramble's wings pulled him toward the ceiling in surprise.

"I learned shortly after becoming a supervisor that it is important to allow the team to work without constant watching. Ms. Swiftwing's job cannot be done with secrets, however."

"Leith will inform me of anything he believes I should know," Maeve's voice said.

Bramble opened his mouth to argue but stopped. Leith's face didn't look like he agreed.

"Let's start with the minister's disappearance," Mamoru said. "What progress have you made?"

Lionel told them what happened at the minister's office. He looked to Rhodri when he was done. That meant he had a secret!

Rhodri didn't say anything for a whole minute. "We obtained a personal object to use in a tracking spell. We will do that and act on the information. It should produce something within a day depending on how many people work on following the leads."

"You can use Briar and Thistle." Bramble wanted his kids to be part of the investigation of the missing minister. The magical corpse was too dangerous.

"Thanks," Lionel said. "The police should be brought in at some point."

"I will manage that," Mamoru said. "You will receive notice. What about the family?"

"The assistant suggested we tread carefully with the family," Rhodri said. "We will follow up with them when the tracking spell gives us a lead."

"They are aware that you are investigating," Maeve's voice said.

Rhodri thanked her and said there was nothing more to report.

"And the murder?" Mamoru asked.

"Leith, you may release the spell. The death of a human is not of interest to me," Maeve's voice announced.

Leith snapped his fingers and told them they were alone again.

"We went to see the autopsy," Bramble said. "We were able to find out what was making the body move around. We need to do some magic to find out if it has some information. We tried at the morgue, but it was too full of dead people to be sure the magic worked right. We will keep trying. We have nothing more to say."

Mamoru nodded. "Agnes, did you gain any insights?"

Why did she need to report? Was she going to say they did something wrong?

"I observed some magic, but I need time to think through the implications. I believe the spell that revealed a little of the murder would be helpful if we can find a way to prove what it shows is not something manipulated."

"Who will you work with next?" Mamoru asked.

"I would like to watch any magic done on that charm, and the tracking spell." Agnes turned to Lionel. "Will it be possible to coordinate the two?"

"The spell is quite simple, it's the follow-up that will take time."

"Then, both I think," she said. "When will you start?"

CHAPTER TWENTY-FIVE

Mamoru left before anyone set up for spell casting. Lionel was glad that Agnes was their only observer. He went to the supply cupboard where the staple ingredients for spells were kept.

"Before you do that, I have some news," Kim said, "on Heath's case."

"That is a secret," Bramble said. "Only for when the team is here. Not Mamoru, not Agnes."

"Well, I know about the investigation now," Agnes said. "Why does this one need to be secret?"

Lionel tried to fade into the background. Bramble was right and wrong. They needed to keep the investigation off the books, but Agnes couldn't be shut out.

"Bramble," Kim said, "we need to talk about the case, and keeping things secret hasn't exactly worked up to now."

"But she will tell Mamoru and then he will tell us to stop." Bramble flew to hang in front of Agnes. "Our friend was killed, and we must find the person responsible. He would still be alive if he hadn't helped us."

"It's not my intention to take sides," Agnes said. "You

know why I'm here, and I need my assessment to be clean if I have any chance of succeeding."

Lionel stepped forward, no longer willing to wait out the argument. "It doesn't make any sense to keep the information from her. Maybe Agnes can help."

Bramble turned on him. "You don't want Heath's murderer punished? But he was a wizard. Why don't you care?"

"I do," Lionel said, patience shredding. He looked around the group for allies. If Bramble fought every time Agnes was involved, nothing would get done. Raj and Leith were too new to know the story. In fact, only Fernlight and Bramble knew everything. "It doesn't matter that he was a wizard. He was murdered. We should care about everyone who is murdered."

"If we tell Mamoru we are investigating, he will stop us. He will tell us again that the new cases are more important. He will always do that. He doesn't care."

Bramble was still speaking, but no one other than his children heard the words because he kept it in the fairy range.

"Agnes said she isn't going to take sides," Lionel said. "Bramble! We can't hear you."

The fairy took a breath. "Fine, she knows we are investigating. Why can't we keep the information secret?"

Lionel recognized his own nervousness in Bramble's eyes. It had been five years, but still humans seemed untrustworthy. Lionel thought he'd gained control over his fear and could treat the humans as equals, but his suspicions surged up the moment trust became most vital.

"If you hide things from me, no one will ever allow magic to be used for investigations," Agnes said. "If you let me observe everything, I will do a better job. And I'll be out of your way sooner."

"But you only want to look at magic," Bramble said. "That's what we agreed to."

"I need to understand why you use different spells. I will be asked about your magic, yes, but also about your approach. Don't you think it will be better if I can say I believe using magic was the right decision?"

"You could just say that," Bramble said.

Lionel relaxed as Bramble's anger faded to hopefulness. Unfortunately, anger would return as quickly if he didn't like the answers.

"No. I have integrity," Agnes said with a smile. "I promise I won't run to Mamoru with every little detail. Doing so won't help me, you, or him."

"You should take an oath," Bramble said. "Then no one would worry about you."

Agnes laughed. "There are two problems with that. First, any hint I might be under magical coercion would destroy my recommendations."

"It would only work to keep you from telling," Bramble said.

"No one would believe that," she answered.

"What's the second problem?" Fernlight asked.

Agnes looked around the room. Everyone seemed engrossed in the discussion. "Trust. If I take the oath, you know I can't tell him anything. But you still won't trust me."

"We need a decision," Kim said. "I have information, and you have spells to cast. Someone needs to say whether we talk freely or not. My vote is to be open with Agnes. If we try to keep the work secret, we'll waste a lot of time and energy that would be better used to find the killers or the minister."

Fernlight moved to the whiteboard. "We work in the open. Either we trust Agnes or we don't. I prefer to think we do because that's the easiest way to keep working. Any arguments?"

No one, not even Bramble, spoke.

"Before you tell us the new information," Fernlight said, "let me bring everyone up to date on the case so far. Maybe a new perspective will help us."

She picked up the marker and wrote out the facts of Heath's murder, talking through the points. It looked pretty sparse. "He was found by the police and we don't know who was behind the murder."

Lionel listened to the case details, hoping to come up with a new idea. When they arrested Birgit Martins, he'd been sure the case had been solved. But there were still some shadows lurking. Some important person giving the orders, and he wondered what kind of important person. Humans gave status for so many things. Maybe a political leader, or a religious one? Or someone with a lot of money? He worried they would never find the real answer. That every time they found the person they thought responsible, they would turn out to be another puppet.

CHAPTER TWENTY-SIX

Hearing the facts didn't help. Bramble fought against his impatience. He understood that if everyone got a chance to understand what happened, they could help more. And sometimes clues came from different cases. But talking felt like a waste of time. It had been five minutes at least since Fernlight started talking.

"And what did you find today?" Leith asked.

Not sidhe business. Bramble expected Leith to only work with them when there was a sidhe problem. But he didn't argue when Fernlight assigned him to the murder and not the missing minister. Things were too complicated when people didn't behave the way he expected.

"Not only me," Kim said. "The brownies. They have a knack for finding links between completely disparate crumbs of information. I guess their abilities give them an edge."

Agnes looked down at the floor beneath the desk. "I'll need to talk to them, too."

"We will answer your questions as long as you do not ask about brownie secrets," Pit said.

Just like brownies. They should tell Agnes everything.

"Let's see what you are going to do before we put walls around the information," she said. "I think everyone is waiting for the clue you found."

Pit climbed up on Kim's desk and nodded at her.

"The company you found, *Sla Styrkur*. It was only part of the name." Kim stood and walked over to the whiteboard.

"Yes," Pit said as she started writing. "The company is called *Sla Styrkur Guðs og örlög*. It's in a language called Icelandic, and the words mean 'beat the strength of god and fate.' This company sounds very important."

Bramble let himself float into his chair. He hadn't expected them to learn that much. With the full name, they should be able to find the criminal today!

"The company is a huge conglomerate," Kim said. "One of the companies made that skin. We are going through a list of the companies it owns, but a lot of them are set up to divert attention. They are numbered companies and registered in a lot of different jurisdictions."

"How will you know when you find the killer?" Bramble asked.

"You can't be sure the killer is connected," Agnes said. "Do you usually jump to conclusions like this?"

"No," Kim said. "We do know a few things that make it probable, but it's not about magic, so why are you asking?"

Agnes smiled. "I'm curious, but are you saying no one will use magic to find the answer?"

"I'm not sure magic will help," Raj said. "This is the kind of work I did in the past. It's going to take a while to sift through the details. I can help if you like."

"Brownies are excellent at finding clues," Pit said. "We do not require help."

Raj smiled the way people do when they want to put other people at ease. Bramble had seen it on one of the Internet places when he was looking for information about how to create a team. Smiling hadn't worked when he tried, but then Raj didn't have as many teeth. Perhaps a fairy smile was for special feelings.

"I'm sure you can do it, Pit," Raj said. "At least let me look at how you are working."

Pit looked at Kim. They were acting like partners. Bramble would talk to Kim later about being careful around tricky brownies.

"We should listen to him," she said. "Even for brownies, corporate structures are convoluted and, if we are right, this one is designed to misdirect investigations."

Pit accepted the offer and restarted his report. "We were able to find some names, but that's when everyone came back, and Mamoru wanted an update so we stopped."

The other brownies could have kept working, Bramble thought.

"Write up the list," Fernlight said. "We should all be looking at the clues in case a name shows up in the other investigations. It happened last time."

"One case is not a good sample," Kim said as she wrote five names on the list. "Although I think it's likely that the pool of suspects in magical crimes is small this early. It won't stay that way."

"Grant Norman, A. Jones, Della Moore, Vivianne Braithwaite, Selwyn Morgan," Bramble read the names aloud. "I have memorized them."

Raj stepped up to the board and took a picture of the information written on it. "I'll share the photo with everyone. In fact, we should always do this with everything. Keep a photo. Not all of us can call things up by magic."

Working with humans was fun and annoying. Fun because taking picture records meant Bramble was able to take photos of everything all the time, and annoying because if humans were not on the team, they wouldn't need to do anything non-magical.

"Okay," Fernlight said. "The brownies and Kim will continue to investigate until they find a clue we can use. Rhodri and Lionel will do a tracking spell and follow the minister's movements. The rest of us will work some spells to try to understand the charm found in the body."

"We will help," Briar said, his sister nudging him. "You said we could help Lionel and Rhodri. We are not afraid of humans. We can help follow the minister around. We..."

"Sorry," Fernlight interrupted the stream. "You are right. Now, any more questions before we cast the circles?"

"I would like to talk a little about how the brownies will work before the magic starts," Agnes said. "And I can't watch two magical demonstrations at the same time."

CHAPTER TWENTY-SEVEN

Her words brought the team to a stop. Agnes wondered if she was expected to sit back and watch what they did without any comment. This was the beginning of the relationship and she needed to start successfully, not try to wrangle them every time a question came up.

"Let's set some expectations," she said. "I guess we've never really talked about how this will work. I keep telling you I'm not here to take sides."

"But you do have a side," Bramble said. He stayed by the whiteboard. "Your side is the way the laws work."

Maybe we come from such different worlds we can't communicate easily. But Kim seems able to do it. And from what I've seen, Bramble accepts Raj more than the brownies or the sidhe.

"I'm also a lawyer," Agnes said. "I can help interpret things for you. And I can tell you where I think things will go badly."

"Like what?" Thistle asked. "Like when we want to make things easy and humans will think we are cheating?"

"You're close," Agnes said. "Even if we weren't dealing with magic, some actions can destroy a case in court. Raj was a private investigator. He will understand some of the challenges."

"Yes. I had to be careful that I didn't let someone think I was a police officer," Raj said. "And I couldn't hack into systems or break into places."

"And most of your work was not going to end up in a criminal case," Kim said. "Even the police work under restrictions."

At least I'm not the only one pushing the button. "Raj, you are right, but we all know you did those things, and it was more about not getting caught."

"We won't be caught," Pit said. He was staring at the monitor with two of his horde pressing keys. "Do you want to understand how we get into places? Well, that's brownie secrets so I won't tell you."

Agnes sighed; they didn't have time for philosophical debates. "Let's talk practicalities. It's not just how you conduct the investigation. You can't go looking for revenge. You need to look at all the facts, not only the ones that fit your theory."

"Revenge is not the same as punishment?" Briar asked. "If we find the person who ordered that lady to kill Heath and we punish them, why is it different if we let the judge and lawyers do the punishing?"

"The judge and lawyers are there to make sure you've found the right person." Raj pointed to the list of names. "Do you think these people are responsible?"

"Yes," Bramble said. "One of them."

"And if you decide one of them did it, how would you punish them?" Raj asked.

"We would put them in a magical prison."

"And if they turned out to be innocent?"

"We do not make mistakes." Bramble fluttered his wings. "But I understand. Humans do make mistakes."

So much for logic.

"We won't solve that today," Agnes said. "I want to make sure you understand one concept before we move on. Then you can decide which order to do your spells in for me to observe."

The team settled behind desks, waiting for her to continue. She reminded herself they wanted to succeed. They just didn't understand that, right now, the human world was trying to bend the magical one to fit. Generations would pass before the two worlds were entwined enough to be equal. Her own people knew how bad things could get. But even without residential schools or internment camps, having your culture and core beliefs dismissed as 'less than' was painful. If she could help a little, it was her responsibility. *Don't talk down. They are not children or mentally deficient.*

"The strongest argument a defense lawyer can make is that the evidence is tainted, and everything learned from that point on is useless. The phrase we use is: 'fruit of the poisoned tree.'"

"So, we need search warrants for every time we want to go into a place?" Lionel asked.

"Or an invitation," Raj said. "One of the benefits of not being on the force is you get some leeway on searches. But you can't simply go in and search."

"Because someone will say we didn't find the clue? That we put the clue in place to find?" Pit asked. "Sneaky. But we have truth spells to make sure it doesn't happen."

"And when we can use the spells, that will help," Agnes said. "But listen to Raj. You can't break in, either to physical or electronic locations."

"Okay," Pit said. "Only if we are invited."

"Or if someone sounds like they are in trouble," Kim said. "If you hear screaming or fighting, you can rush in to rescue someone."

"We are too small for rescues." Pit looked away from the screen. "Perhaps some of you are big enough. If we can find things on the marvelous Internet, is that breaking in?"

"Don't trust everything you learn there," Raj said. "So, any more questions? I'm looking forward to some magic."

No one had any more questions, and Agnes hoped it wasn't because they were busy plotting how to maneuver around her restrictions. She didn't need to get it right the first time, but she hoped for something less than a disaster.

"Which spell comes first?" she asked.

CHAPTER TWENTY-EIGHT

This time Agnes was going to be in a magical circle. She had seen magic before, but it was very different to simply observe than it was to assess the legal use of it. This time an air of excited anticipation had her stomach quivering. The beads were magic and the spells around her would be the same. The feeling wasn't fear, but a tinge of worry. Would this be the feeling every time? Her nerves might not survive, but she hoped it never got boring and ordinary.

Lionel stood with a string crusted in salt. "Sit closer together, please. I don't want to make a giant circle. Briar, Thistle, settle."

Thistle landed on Agnes's shoulder with a small humph of indignation. Briar chose to stand on the dirt between her and Rhodri.

"Agnes, I'm going to enclose us in the circle and then we'll try some spells on the beads. You might feel a little pressure when I seal the protections."

"Do you always do this in a circle?" she asked. Her recommendations would be enhanced by any knowledge she could glean. It was freeing to learn something she would never be able to use. All theory and no practice.

"For some spells," Lionel said as he started laying the string out. "Not usually something like this, or the spells they will cast on the amulet. But it's better not to be distracted if you are going to assess us."

He crossed the ends of the string and the air thickened, not enough to pop her ears, but close. She no longer heard noises from the office beside them, so she just waited.

Rhodri pulled a few seeds and nuts from his pocket and laid them on the ground.

"What about fairy magic?" Thistle asked. Her voice was blunted by the spell.

"If we don't learn anything from these, or the earth magic, we'll try," Lionel said. "But you need to keep track of the locations the spell uncovers."

"Okay," Briar said. "Let's get going."

"We'll start with the charms," Rhodri said. "These are spells to uncover lost facts. It should show us a list of locations. After that, we'll try Lionel's spells."

"Does every type of magical folk use a different spell?"

"Yes, but they all work in the same way. I don't think you need to observe a tracking spell from every type of being. Here, we will show you three."

I'll decide how far I need to range in my report. "Why are you doing three if they all work the same way?" she asked.

"Ah," Rhodri said. "I wasn't clear enough. They all work the same from a magical point of view in that they don't damage the item and they seek in the past. My magic will list the locations. Lionel's magic will produce a smoke we can follow from one to the other. Fairy magic will show images of what the minister saw in each place."

Combinations that would be handy for every investigator, Agnes thought.

"I'll keep any questions for after you've done your spell."

Lionel took the beads out of the small box and put them in the center of the circle. The atmosphere thickened a little more, and queasiness slithered in her gut. Briar floated off the ground and landed on Agnes's knee.

"That's new," Lionel said. "It shouldn't affect the circle. Maybe you can ask the earth spirits to check it out?"

Rhodri placed his hands on the earth and his tattoos darkened. Agnes made a note to ask why. After a moment, he removed his hands and leaned in to look closer at the beads. This was the first time anyone had glowed after magic. She wished she could ask questions, and she hated holding onto them. Was that coercion? Would she even know when she was being used?

"It is not a protection spell," Rhodri said. "Someone placed a dissension spell on the beads. Give me a moment."

He placed his hands on the earth again. An indentation appeared below the beads and then a pop released the pressure in Agnes's head.

"What happened?" she asked.

"We all felt it. I think you suspected us of something. Is it gone?" Lionel asked. When Agnes nodded, he continued, "The circle must have amplified the power. This was supposed to be part of Feng Shui. A protection."

"The spell is harmless now. The power sunk into the earth. It will do no harm there. It is simply power."

"Will it have an impact on the tracking spell?" Agnes was invested in the magic working; this agency and future victims of magic crimes depended on her report. All the suspicion she felt earlier was gone now that the beads were just wooden objects untainted with a spell.

"No," Thistle said. "At least, not with fairy magic. It might even help if the minister kept getting mad at people. If he did, more of his essence will be used up."

That was a relief. Whatever magic they'd used to obtain the string of beads was worth it. Agnes was happy to stay ignorant on that front.

"Shall we continue?" Lionel asked. "Start with the charms."

Rhodri broke the seeds and nuts one at a time. Smoke rose and spelled out places she recognized around the city. Briar called them out and Thistle wrote them on a scrap of paper.

The wizard spell raised a finger of smoke that fell apart as it hit the dome of protection, and the fairy spell showed images of the places already listed.

"Did you see enough?" Rhodri asked. "We will need to follow these leads and try the spells at different locations."

The beads looked the same. Agnes felt no compulsion to decide one way or another. "I agree that you can track from magic. I'll reserve my final recommendation for the results. Are you going to talk to the assistant again?"

"Not yet," Lionel said. "Perhaps the brownies could go and check if she's still there and if there's any residue of the dissension spell."

"It's a public office," Agnes said. "They won't need to sneak in."

Lionel lifted the string of beads to put them back in the container. When he touched them, he jerked his hand back. "The disruption spell is recharging. I don't like that idea. It should have died completely." He untwisted the ends of the salt string. "We should keep the beads in the box. I'm not sure that they are safe. Fernlight and Bramble will cast their own circle. This salt string needs to be recharged."

An hour later, Agnes stood and stretched. This time the spells were less visual and also far less successful. Bramble and

Fernlight huddled together discussing the lack of details and making plans for future magic. Agnes needed her bed.

CHAPTER TWENTY-NINE

They were back at the morgue. Bramble was not as scared this time, at least not as badly. Still too many dead humans for his comfort, but Doctor Phillips was friendlier, and his assistant didn't glare at him so much. Maybe they liked the morning better. It had been a whole day since Mamoru showed them where the body hung, and Bramble hoped they could solve this case today.

"Thank you for coming so quickly," Doctor Phillips said. "We have some results."

Bramble stayed close to Fernlight, keeping his attention separated between the doctor and Leith in case the sidhe did something sneaky. Raj and Agnes stood a bit apart. Raj shouldn't do that. He was part of the team.

And Agnes shouldn't be here. They weren't going to do magic.

"Will your results lead to finding the killer?" Leith asked.

"We have an identity, so that might help," Milo, the assistant, said. "We don't go looking for the criminals. That's your job."

"Why didn't you just tell us on the phone?" Fernlight said. "Why are we here?"

"There are details about the body I wanted you to look at," Doctor Phillips said. "Perhaps you can shed some light on the causes."

"Just show us," Bramble said. "We need to go out and catch the person who did the murder."

The doctor took a deep breath and looked down at the sheet covering the body. "I am not used to being questioned," he said. "And I am not used to magic, so perhaps I am stalling. The victim's name is Ivan Sawchuk, mid to late thirties, no piercings, six tattoos, no evidence of previous trauma. According to the police, no criminal record and no obvious ties to any criminal activity."

"You told the police?" Bramble asked. *This is our case!*

"My cousin is a cop," Milo said. "I thought I'd give you a head start."

"Do the tats point us anywhere?" Raj asked. "Did your cousin tell you anything else?"

"He's one of those graphic artists in his spare time," Milo said. "Did freelance, book covers, album covers, brands. That kind of stuff."

"I made copies of the tattoos. You'll find them in the file," Doctor Phillips said. "Maybe you can find out who did them."

They are being very helpful, Bramble thought.

"Is there more you wanted to show us?" Fernlight asked. "We will need to look at the tattoos and use a spell or two to see if we can find anything. I assume since your tests are done, you won't mind us using magic."

"Actually, yes. And I'm stumped and worried this is only the first. Do you think anyone will be interested in consulting for us? In a magical sense."

"Before you do anything like that, I need to put in my

recommendations," Agnes said. "Why don't we look at what you found before we delve into casting spells?"

Since he'd promised Fernlight he would stop fighting about Agnes's job, Bramble didn't say anything aloud about her being a problem. There was no point in doing magic until they saw the body again anyway. And maybe she would help them more than she got in the way.

Doctor Phillips told Milo to remove the sheet and then beckoned them to the body. It didn't smell so bad now. The rotting was still tainting the air, but all the cleaning helped.

It surprised Bramble the body wasn't covered in bruises from all the dancing around. The body, where it wasn't scratched or punctured, looked fine.

"As you can see, our initial thought that this was a junkie is probably not right. While Mr. Sawchuk was not in the best of shape, he isn't wasted. No signs of malnutrition, or the usual parasites and infections we expect from long-term drug use."

"But he is covered in puncture marks," Raj said, "and not insect bites. I recognize injection sites."

"Yes," Doctor Phillips said. "The needle marks were all made in the last couple of days. If this was about drugs, Mr. Sawchuk would have been dead by the tenth injection."

"Is there magic that will do this?" Raj asked.

Leith stepped closer to the body. "Some older rites might cause this much damage. Rhodri, or any of the other druids could tell you more, but I've done some research in my time." He looked at Doctor Phillips and then pointed to a cluster of the holes. "One of the rites is a purification. A thread is drawn through the skin and left. The subject waits until the thread begins to rot and must draw out each stitch while listing the acts leading up to the rite."

"Sounds like religious purification," Raj said.

"No, it is deep magic that restores an extremely damaged

spirit. But I haven't heard of anyone doing it for at least five hundred years. And even then, it was a banshee rite."

"If that was the reason, we'd see infection lines where the thread had rotted. These are definitely puncture marks." Doctor Phillips moved on to the head and turned it. "Look here. More damage to the skin, but not punctures. Burns."

Bramble didn't know any magic that did so much damage. Fairies were not so cruel. Maybe the sidhe were, because Leith knew a lot. "Should we ask the druids to come look?"

"I was thinking druids would be a good source of consultants," Fernlight said, "but not yet. Do we have pictures of all this?"

"In the file." Doctor Phillips turned the head so it faced up again.

"Are you going to do magic?" Milo asked. "Like, see what caused the damage? Now that the charm is gone?"

Fernlight stared at the body for a while before looking up and saying, "It would be helpful if we tried the same spell as before. But this time only on certain patches of skin. We might be able to find out what caused the holes and burns."

"It's definitely a needle," Doctor Phillips said.

"But was it a metal one, or a bone one, or some kind of reed?" Bramble asked, looking at Agnes. "The answer might be a clue."

"If Doctor Phillips has no objections, I won't stand in the way."

The spell gave them no more information than before. Raj took the file and Bramble followed everyone out of the room, disappointed and frustrated at the lack of clues.

CHAPTER THIRTY

When they arrived back at the office, Bramble flitted to the whiteboard and wrote Ivan Sawchuk's name. He didn't know how it would help because Kim was the only one who could use the police database, and she needed to be working on Heath's case.

"We need to do some research on this man now that we know his name," Fernlight said. "Kim, can you give Raj access? This is a human tool, and it will be faster for a human to do the work."

Excellent idea.

"I need a second sign-in account," Kim said. "If Raj is using mine, I can't use it at the same time."

Bramble grabbed his phone off the desk where he'd left it by mistake. "I will call Mamoru. He will give us more codes. He should give us enough for the whole team."

No one tried to stop him, so Bramble made the call. He put it on speaker so the others could hear how well he managed to make Mamoru help.

"I have a better solution," Mamoru said when Bramble explained.

"We just need codes. Our solution is the best."

"I think it is important that the human and magical teams understand how the other works. Send two team members here to HOP-D to access the records."

"But Kim is teaching us," Fernlight said. "And Raj. We are learning how the humans investigate."

"It is too big a job for Kim to do," Mamoru said. "And the current situation does not allow my human investigators to see how magical folk work."

"This was not our agreement," Fernlight said. Now her voice was firm, and Bramble was glad she wasn't speaking to him. "We investigate the magical crimes. We do not need to understand how your current employees do their work."

Mamoru didn't answer right away. Bramble hoped he realized that Fernlight was right. But what would they do if Mamoru said he didn't want to work with them anymore? They had been open almost a whole day without a client when he came to them.

"I remember our agreement clearly. Experience shows there is no separate magical crime," Mamoru said finally. "The legal system is human. Agnes is there to help you. Two people for just this one task. You need the work done, and I can't continue to be the go-between."

"You are trying to make us work at HOP-D," Bramble shouted. He hadn't meant to say anything, but he was too afraid to work there. It was too far from the earth for Rhodri, and for anyone who needed power.

"No," Mamoru said, "I do not believe this is the right location for you. But I have come to think that you need to work with us more closely and we need to work with you. When Agnes finishes her recommendations, we will find ways for you to help on our investigations."

He already changed the agreement once. How would Bramble make sure his tribe was safe without the work from the agency? His plan seemed to be set only a few minutes ago. Now he was back to worrying that the Bramble tribe would fade away.

He looked to Fernlight, hoping she would find a way to stop this.

"Two people," she said. "I will send you Leith and Raj, but only for as long as it takes to find our information."

"Three hours," Mamoru said. "Time to find everything you need, and they will meet my other investigators. And they will talk about magical investigating."

"Three hours," Fernlight agreed. "And we will discuss this integration you plan. Do not assume we will simply agree."

"Are you still sure you want Raj and Leith?"

"Yes. Raj has seen us work and knows human investigations. Leith understands the political considerations and he's investigated for Maeve in the past."

"Very well. I'll expect them in a half hour." Mamoru ended the call.

"I am not going to work in that building," Rhodri said.

"None of us want that," Lionel said. "We will wither in an office. Too far from nature. Difficult to maintain power levels."

"Brownies will not mind," Pit said. "We do not expect to be inside any office for long times."

They spend a lot of hours in this office.

"Worrying about it will only get in the way of the cases," Kim said. "I'm not going to work in HOP-D headquarters either. We'll figure something out."

Yes, they would. Bramble's wings trembled with joy. He would not be alone if he had to leave the agency. And a few hours without a sidhe patronizing him would be nice.

CHAPTER THIRTY-ONE

Three hours? Why does it need to take so long? Bramble flew around the room, staying close to the ceiling so he didn't need to dodge anyone. He could find information with a spell in three minutes. Now they had to wait, and the case was dragging, and they couldn't even help with the minister case because Lionel was with Rhodri and the kids following the spells. And the brownies would be better at finding all the hidden information on Heath's case.

Wait! Mamoru didn't say they had to sit still. They could still do the spell. He stopped his flight and looked around the room. Fernlight was talking to Kim. Agnes was writing something in her notebook. If he went quietly, did the spell in the casting room, and came back with the information they needed, everyone would be happy. And the sidhe wouldn't be the hero who came back with the answers. He drifted toward the door to the room they used as a workshop. Everything he needed was in there.

"Bramble, what are you going to do?" Agnes called out.

He fought with his wings. They didn't want to stop but he knew Agnes wouldn't forget what she'd seen.

"We can still do a spell to find out about the victim's family and friends." He was careful not to make it a question. She would never say yes if he asked permission.

"Is this a spell I've seen before?" She stood to join him.

"No." He noticed Fernlight watching. And Kim. What happened to fairies being sneaky? At least the brownies didn't look at him. They were concentrating on their job. "I was going to ask a spirit to give us the information."

"Spirits are not fairy magic," Fernlight said. "The spell would work better on a person."

"Yes, but I didn't want to ask because I didn't think it was nice to use one of our human team members for testing." He was sure Raj would say yes because he was fun, but not Kim because she already knew what it was like, or Agnes because she was supposed to be watching them.

"Tell me what the spell does to the person," Agnes said. "I don't want to wait until we hear from Raj or Leith either."

"I can show you," Bramble said. "I can cast the spell on you and then you will tell us the names." *What a great idea. She will know how magic feels and be less scared.*

Agnes shook her head. "I can't let you cast a spell on me. It will invalidate my work and you'll have to start again. With someone else."

"Kim?" Fernlight asked. "Would you be willing? The brownies are doing most of the research right now."

Kim rolled her chair away from the desk. "Is it going to hurt?"

"No," Bramble said. Well, no one had complained before. But they had all been fairies and going through the ritual that changed them from fairy babies to fairy adults. "It will only take a little time and when we are done, you will be just the same as you are now."

"I don't have many relatives," she said. "But what about friends? Like only if I think they are friends?"

"Don't you like all your friends?" Bramble asked. Humans were strange.

"Some people might think they are my friends but are really only acquaintances."

"We'll see," Fernlight said. "Most magical folk don't have those relationships."

"It will mean something different if the spell only gives you the names of my friends. And I wonder if I'll find relatives I don't know about."

"And how will this demonstration work for the victim?" Agnes asked. "It's fine to see this work, but the victim is dead. You won't be able to ask him."

"That's why I was going to ask the spirits!" Bramble said. "I didn't want to put it on Kim. I want to do the spell in a circle with a spirit. The whole thing looks easy when Lionel does it. I know they want candy. I don't want anyone else in there in case something goes wrong."

"There is another way," Fernlight said. "I don't want you talking to the spirits without an expert in the circle. But we can use clothing from the victim. It won't be perfect, but it would be a start."

"We don't have anything like that!" Bramble's wings pulled him up to the ceiling in frustration. And it was getting too hard to keep his voice in the non-fairy range.

"No, but we could get them," Fernlight said. "The brownies can retrieve them if Doctor Phillips agrees."

"Yes. We can be delivery brownies," Pit said from his computer. "That is another business we can start if you need to go work in HOP-D. We can take things and bring things but not stay in that building."

Kim picked up her phone and sent a text. It was like a fairy message, short and not too many words.

"I know him," she said. "He'll want to cooperate. He's

kind of a new toy junkie. And he sees magic as a whole bag of new toys."

Her phone beeped. "You can go now. He'll give you the shoes. Will that be okay?"

Not just okay. Perfect. "Yes. Explain what the brownies are so he doesn't worry."

"Pit, who's going?" Kim asked.

"Shade will do it. She will take ten of our horde with her." He didn't look away from the screen.

"Shade, hop up here," Kim said, patting the top of her desk. "I'll send him your picture. No. Don't dance or make faces like that. Be still and look at me."

When she sent the picture, Kim told Shade where the parcel would be, and the brownies left.

"Can we try the spell anyway?" Kim asked. "You might need to use something like it in the future, and Agnes can include the results in her recommendations."

Bramble found a few laurel leaves in the supply closet. He used his own power and shreds of the leaves to cast the spell. Kim's eyes went distant and then she started listing names. Fernlight recorded the results. When Kim stopped speaking, Bramble released the spell.

"I'm fine," Kim said to Agnes. "I kind of zoned out. I heard myself talking but couldn't stop."

She looked at the list of names. "Okay. For the record, I apparently have a cousin living in Surrey. Two of the names on the list of friends are a surprise — I thought they were just colleagues. Can't explain why. No one is missing as far as I can tell."

Bramble looked on the list. He was the first name of all the team members Kim said were friends.

CHAPTER THIRTY-TWO

Lionel opened the door to the office. He'd left Rhodri and the fairy kids following the minister's tracks because there were not enough locations to need all of them. He planned on digging into the minister's public life on the Internet.

The office was quiet. Plenty of people and no arguments. He tried to see that as a benefit.

"Lionel, you are here!" Bramble said. "Did you find him? Where are Briar and Thistle, where is Rhodri?"

He explained quickly and went to his desk. Fernlight joined him and beckoned to Bramble.

"Agnes is busy trying to think of questions about the last spell," Fernlight said. "Since we have nothing on the other cases, we thought we'd look at Heath's notebook again."

"Did Kim find something?" Lionel's hopes crashed as soon as he spoke. Neither of them was smiling.

"We thought of a spell to use," Bramble said. "All this talk of spell casting and explaining made me think of a way to find clues. But we need a wizard to do it. We can't use wizard magic."

"You plan on sneaking into the back room?" Lionel asked. He had no doubt that there were secrets in Heath's spell book. Finding them might not reveal any more clues but would increase his knowledge. Heath was a wizard who liked to experiment widely. Lionel didn't care for the risk inherent in more than testing out simple spells, but he did want the results of Heath's work.

"We are not using magic on a person," Fernlight said. "Only on a magic book. When we find the killer, no one will care."

That's the exact opposite of what Agnes explained. But did it matter? When they found the person who ordered the death of a wizard, he or she would be important and influential. Lionel had read enough articles about powerful people slipping through the human legal system to lose his faith in their ability to get justice that way.

"And what will we do when we find them?" he asked. Anyone else he would be happy to imprison like Quinn had Fionuir. But this person would be missed. Perhaps no one knew about the murder, but it was unlikely they always operated in the shadows.

"You don't want to arrest him?" Bramble asked. He looked over at Agnes and Kim who were huddled over a drawing of magical items. "The wizards have a prison?"

"No." Lionel moved toward the door to the spell room. "Let's do it now."

Inside, Lionel created the circle and then waited. When no one spoke, he said, "You had an idea?"

Bramble popped up from the ground where he'd been waiting for Lionel to start talking to Heath's book. "Oh. I forgot we didn't tell you. I thought that if you explained to the book that Heath was dead and we needed information to help catch the person, and then you cast a spell to seek information, the book might be helpful to us."

"The book is just a book," Lionel said. "It doesn't make choices."

Fernlight waved Bramble to the ground again. "Yes, but what if there is a spell set to reveal the secrets when Heath dies?"

"Normally when a wizard dies, one of two things happen with their spell library. Usually, everything goes to an apprentice."

"But Heath didn't have an apprentice," Bramble said.

"The other option is that it simply stays locked up." Revealing a wizard's private spell library to anyone who opened the book was dangerous. But most wizards took at least one apprentice.

"Heath worked with humans," Fernlight reminded him. "Very closely with them. I think it affected the way he thought about his magic."

"He was determined to make magic like a tool, or at least some of it." Bramble rose and started flitting around the circle. "So, I think he would want someone to find the work and continue. I think if we can pull the secrets out, they will help us find the killer, and we can continue his work, or you can, or someone else."

Now that the opportunity was in front of him, Lionel saw the logic. If he had such a spell, would he restrict it tightly, or would any magical folk be able to access the contents? He didn't have many spells to share and had already arranged for Dionne to access the spells on his death.

If Bramble was right, Heath still wouldn't leave his knowledge wide open. Maybe he would have set certain conditions. He knew what Fernlight and Bramble were doing with the detective agency so it wasn't a stretch to assume they would be part of the key. But he would need a wizard to cast the spell. A spell the wizard needed to figure out.

"It's worth a try," Lionel said. "Heath was pretty new to

Vancouver. I only saw him a couple of times in Banks'. If I can't make this work, we should try Quinn or Dionne. Heath would know of them at least."

"So why are we still talking about it?" Bramble buzzed one more circle then landed on the ground. "How do we start?"

"I think one of you needs to explain the situation. He would have trusted you both and so used that in the spell to protect the contents."

"But our magic is not wizard magic," Bramble said.

"I think Lionel is right." Fernlight placed the book in the center of the floor. "Our part is to wake up the spell. I don't know any other way to explain. Lionel will do the magic; we need to set the conditions."

Lionel cleared his mind as Fernlight spoke. She understood spell casting much more than he expected. He closed his eyes and let the doubts settle. When all he felt was peace, he opened his eyes and nodded.

Bramble and Fernlight touched the book cover as they introduced Lionel and explained the situation. As their words dropped away, a gentle pressure rested on his forehead.

Please reveal your secrets.

The pressure released and Heath's voice startled them.

"I guess I'm dead. I figured it was a possibility, but hoped I was wrong. So, you can hear me. That means Fernlight and Bramble are there, and one of the local wizards.

"I don't know who killed me, or why, let's get that clear. But the wizard will be able to read and perform any spell in the book or any of my books.

"I've deeded my home to whoever can cast the spell to reveal the paperwork. It's in here if you look hard enough.

"I'm dead, so I can only ask this next favor. When it's safe, can you continue my work? I truly believe magic will help bind our two worlds together.

"That's all. You won't hear from me again. Sorry I was careless and can't work on any other investigations."

The words cut off and then the spell book flipped open.

CHAPTER THIRTY-THREE

Lionel had Heath's book open on his desk. So many spells he'd never considered. And he had a home! Not that living with Quinn was a problem; it wasn't unusual for an apprentice to stay with his mentor for a while after achieving his wizard standing. But now there was an option, he wanted the solitude to study. And all the spells and equipment at Heath's were now his. Excitement and dreaming of possibilities dragged his attention from gleaning clues.

"Wizard Lionel." Pit stood on the desk staring at the book like it was a candy.

"You can just call me Lionel. I'm the only one with that name."

"And if we encounter another Lionel? What do we call him?"

The brownie started pulling papers from his bag. The magic allowing him to carry a tote that could hold a ream of papers and a phone was similar to fairy magic that allowed Bramble to change his size.

"We'll think about that later. What do you have there?" Lionel nodded toward the stack of papers.

"What we found on all the businesses owned by that company. We want to make a presentation, but not everyone is here."

Lionel looked around the office. Agnes was alone at a desk, reading her phone. Bramble and Fernlight were talking with Kim. Would it make a difference if Raj, Leith, and Rhodri missed the report?

"I think you should wait," he said, "until Agnes has gone home."

"Will she not find our results interesting? Is it because of the brownie magic?" Pit looked down to the floor and made a stopping motion with his hand. Lionel stood and leaned over to see the horde retreating under the desk.

"A little," he said. "I don't think she believes your magic allows you to enter places without breaking in. She thinks of you like humans still. Well, all of us really. It will take her a while, I think, to realize we are much more different from humans than just having magic."

"But we should show her, so she learns. It is not efficient to let her think too long without facts."

Not the only reason. "Maybe, but that should be a group decision. And I am afraid if she sees how much work is being done on Heath's case, she might let Mamoru know."

"And he will stop us," Pit said. "I did not think of that. Agnes is not the only one who needs to understand differences. We are capable of doing much more than these three cases, yes?"

Lionel wasn't sure. When the team settled in, maybe. But if the brownies did more research, perhaps all the cases would benefit from their help. Something to talk to Fernlight about.

"Give the new team members a little time to integrate," Lionel said. "I have a feeling we are going to find far more cases with magic involvement. We will need to work together more in the future."

Pit puffed himself up. "The brownies are happy to work hard. We will be making more businesses in our spare time."

It must be nice to have an entire horde at your disposal.

"Do you think you found something that can't wait?" Lionel considered a spell to nudge Agnes to work from home. Then cursed himself. They would never be independent if they cheated. It was hard to stop the impulse to use magic. If Heath was still alive, maybe things would be different. His magical tools would help immensely in getting humans to understand.

"It is hard to say without everyone's mind focused on the details," Pit said. "We found lists of people, and companies. We found all of them. And industries. Did you know about industries?"

"What are they?"

"Groups of businesses all producing the same kind of thing. Like there is an industry for farming, and for making things, and for war. So many of them."

An excellent way to organize. All companies in one industry working together. "Are the companies all from the same industry?"

"No. But more information will need to wait until we report. I am ready when the time is right." Pit moved to leave the desk.

"Wait," Lionel said. "If I made a list of all the spells, could the horde look for meaning?"

He pointed to the screen where he had started a spread-sheet of the spells in Heath's book.

Pit joined Lionel to look at the screen. "Very good. Yes, we can find meaning. Can we read the book?"

Lionel opened it to a random page. If the brownies went through the pages, all the better.

"The page is blank," Pit said. "Finish the list, and we will think about what data you need to put in for us to analyze."

Disappointment dragged at Lionel. Normally he would have delighted in culling every iota of information from the book. Normally he would do it in his library with nothing else demanding his attention. But that would wait. "Tell me when you need the spreadsheet," he said.

Pit nodded and then climbed down to join the horde on the floor.

CHAPTER THIRTY-FOUR

The shoes sat in a cardboard box on Kim's desk. Bramble stared at them, hoping for a hint about their secrets. The only things he sensed were a bad smell and more dirt than shoe.

"Doctor Phillips and Milo sent this, too," Pit said. He held up a plastic bag with a sliver of wood covered in blood. "It is from the crime scene. I said we might need to practice the spell on something, so he gave us this."

"Thank you, Pit," Fernlight said. "Good idea, since the last time we used magic on this case, we learned nothing."

Pit beamed. "We went to the crime scene. No one noticed us. If you need more of this kind of evidence, we can collect wood, dirt, rope, bricks. So many pieces all over the place."

Bramble looked to where Agnes was talking to Kim. He didn't think she had overheard Pit's offer. "Don't say that kind of thing when she is around," he hissed, nodding to Agnes. She looked up as though suddenly aware they were keeping secrets.

"If we are not successful, perhaps Mamoru can arrange for us to conduct a spell or two at the site," Fernlight said.

Agnes joined them. Bramble turned back to Pit, but he was gone. *Sneaky brownies.*

"Are we ready to start?" she asked.

Kim came over to watch too. *Why are the humans so curious?*

"Where did you get the splinter?" Kim reached for the bag, but Bramble jerked it away. "You can't take things from the crime scene."

"The brownies asked Doctor Phillips for something we could test before we did the real investigative magic." Bramble didn't like protecting Pit, but he wasn't going to slow the case by blaming anyone.

"Are we going into a circle?" Agnes asked. "What are the spell components?"

"Yes," Bramble said. "We will do this in a circle, so nothing escapes. I will do the magic." Why did she keep asking questions? She should just observe.

"And the ingredients?" Agnes persisted. "I don't want any magic secrets, but I notice you use everyday items in the spells. If I can give any information that the courts can understand, it will help. I promise."

"Who is the courts?" Bramble asked. He picked up the bag, leaving the shoebox on the desk for safety. "Only Agnes will join me in the circle."

"The courts aren't a person," Kim said. "It's a process."

Bramble led them into the spell room. Fernlight stayed in the office, but Kim tagged along. "How does a process understand anything?"

"The people involved in the process need to understand," Agnes said. "The judges, the Crown Council and the defense."

"What crown?" Bramble asked. He took rosemary and sage from the cupboard and a small jug of pure water.

Agnes sighed. "Criminal offenses here are considered crimes against the queen."

He placed the ingredients in the middle of the floor and buzzed over to pick a fresh salt string. "You have a queen?"

Kim laughed. "No. She is the queen of another country. It's very complicated, Bramble. It probably makes more sense for you to look the information up. But you can do it later; nothing you'll find is important to this."

"Okay," he said. "Are you staying?"

Kim sat and motioned for Agnes to do the same. "Yes. I thought it would be good if I understood some of the magic stuff. I might be able to suggest some spells in the future. Use my investigative skills to point out what information we need, and you do the spells."

"And you are curious," he said. "Please do not ask questions while we do this magic."

"What about as you prepare?" Agnes said. She had a pen in her hand and a pad of paper on her knee. "I would appreciate some warning of what we are going to experience."

If they weren't here, I could have cast the spell ten times by now.

He paused his thoughts so his words would be patient. "The reason I don't want you to talk when I am doing the magic is because I could lose concentration and spoil everything. Do not ask anything after I tell you to stop. Okay?"

Kim and Agnes nodded.

"You can see that I am using rosemary and sage for the spell. I also have pure water to clean the blood if I need to. The fairy magic will make the blood and wood answer my questions. The rosemary is to help it to remember important things. The sage will clear out any bad spirits before we open the circle again."

"Have you used sweetgrass for that?" Agnes asked. "It's much like our smudging ceremonies. Some use sage, some sweetgrass."

"This is not the same," Bramble said. "We use sweetgrass for other things."

"There's a Ph.D. thesis in there somewhere. The connections between magical herb uses and indigenous rites." Agnes made a note.

"If you want to talk about that, the druids will welcome you," Bramble said. "I am almost ready. Do you have any other questions?" *Hopefully not.*

"What are we trying to learn?" Kim asked.

"I will ask two questions. First, who knows this dead man. And then, I will ask if the murderer is a magical person. I'm sure it's not, but you think it might be, right?"

"Yes," Agnes said. "Not because I want it to be, but humans don't do magic."

Bramble frowned at her. The last case was proof that humans could use magic even if they couldn't do any without help. "I don't expect much from the first question, but if you write down any names that come up it will be very useful when we use the shoes."

Agnes agreed, and Kim grinned then pretended to zip her lips closed.

Bramble sealed the circle. "No more questions or any speaking."

He shook the bloody wood out of the bag. He placed the sage to the side and took three needles of rosemary and bruised them. Placing the fragrant spikes in a triangle around the wood, he drew on his magic.

"I wish to know who is family with the man who lost the blood."

A trace of steam floated up and spelled out Dominic Stenmark, then collapsed back to float around the wood. Bramble waited for a whole minute before deciding there were no more names coming.

"I wish to know who knows the man who lost the blood or is his friend."

Even if he only had one relative, Ivan must have had

friends. Bramble used the special emphasis on the word that would include anyone who might like the man.

The mist rose again and started writing. A long list of names appeared. Bramble heard Agnes writing them down, so he thought about what next to ask. It was no use asking if the killer was a magical folk because all the names were human.

They would try the spell on the shoes, but blood was a good magic conductor. There was only one other question to try.

"Tell me the name of the killer," Bramble said.

One letter only, and that disintegrated before it was complete. The blood was losing its connection to the man. The shoes would be stronger. But the blood and wood had one strength they didn't; if this time it didn't work, Pit could bring more. The sliver had been there when Ivan died.

"I wish to know who killed the man who lost the blood." He pushed more fairy power toward the spell.

The mist rose again. This time it drew a picture. Still the same as they saw in the morgue. This was from a different angle. The killer dragging Ivan's body still showed, but nothing to identify him.

Bramble lit the sage and waved the smoke around to fill the circle. He doused the remaining stems in the water and opened the circle.

"Disappointing," Kim said.

CHAPTER THIRTY-FIVE

Lionel turned the page in Heath's notebook. His mind struggled to absorb anything he read now. Heath didn't look at magic in the same way as Quinn, and he felt like he was becoming the apprentice again.

Rhodri pulled a chair to join him at the desk. "We have some results," he said. Then when Lionel just blinked at him, he added, "From the tracking spell."

"Oh. I guess nothing about where the minister is?" The missing human fell below the study of Heath's magic for a moment. If they closed the case, Lionel might be able to visit his new home.

"There are a number of people we can interview," Rhodri said. "We followed up on the locations from the spell. Many are in busy commercial areas. It is possible someone saw the minister and isn't on the list. We can go into shops and ask, discreetly of course."

"I need to talk to Agnes first," Lionel said. He still carried guilt from sneaking off to do the spell. If she knew that the book might contain useful magic, perhaps she would want to see what the brownies find.

Fernlight joined them and looked over Lionel's shoulder to the spreadsheet on the screen. "You should go now," she said. "Don't give Agnes any reason to stop you."

Paranoia wasn't going to solve cases. "How many witnesses?" he asked Rhodri.

"Can we have the brownies?" Rhodri asked instead of giving him the number. "They can search around while we talk. The kids can take all the notes we need."

"They are working on this and the companies that connect to *Sla Styrkur*, and all these new spells," Lionel said.

"Pit," Fernlight called.

"Yes. I heard them talking. I am too busy. Shade will come."

Lionel touched the book. It would be safe here. No one could open the covers, and even if they somehow managed it, the true secrets were safe. He slid it into his pocket, reluctant to be parted from his new knowledge.

"Where do we start?" he asked as he walked to the front door.

"It doesn't matter," Rhodri said. "We were unable to determine what location is the first or the last. This case is full of odd happenings. I must say that my fellow druids will be fascinated with all the complications."

Lionel's experience was too shallow to make him certain, but he suspected it had something to do with the string of beads charm. The spell had been in their office and might be the reason everything was muddled and failing. "Should we return the stolen charm?"

"We can't be sure that it is clear of the compulsions," Rhodri said. "You think the magic is affecting us?"

"Don't you?" Lionel lost the shred of doubt. If Rhodri thought the same, then his suspicion was likely right. "Do you think we can clear the spell?"

"Unless it's drawing power back, we should be safe,"

Rhodri said. "I wish passing the power to the earth meant the spell dissipated too. If we make no headway today, perhaps we will take it to the museum. Trahaearn may know of a cleansing spell or have a safer storage place. But no, I don't think we should return the charm to the minister's office. No one there has any protection against the spell if it should regain power."

Lionel couldn't bring himself to feel optimistic about progress.

CHAPTER THIRTY-SIX

"The air should be clean enough now," Bramble announced. He'd delayed doing the spell on the shoes for a while because he wanted the sadness in his mind to go away from the last try. If he didn't go into the next spell with happiness, things would go wrong. Even Fernlight had believed him when he said he needed the sage smoke to be gone. He trusted his partner, but this was fairy magic, and she was a sprite.

Now they will find the killer and Agnes will say that magic is the best tool. And she will go away and tell Mamoru not to worry about any spells they wanted to do.

"Is this time going to be different?" Kim asked. "I like seeing you do magic, but I have things to do if the spell is the same."

She is not happy enough to join us in the circle. Bramble remembered at the last second to keep the thoughts inside. Kim might be offended because she didn't understand. He needed to do everything he could think of to make the magic work right. He also didn't want a repeat of the spell on the wood and blood.

"It will show more, but not any different," he said.

"I'll pass," she said and turned back to the computer.

Fernlight and Agnes joined him in the workroom.

"Do you need anything more than last time?" Agnes asked. "I can help with the ingredients. That seems quite mundane."

Bramble asked her to find the freshest rosemary and to make a bigger bundle of sage to burn. "The magic is stronger," he said, "so we need to use more cleansing smoke."

"I'll make the circle," Fernlight said. "You just sit in the center until we are ready. That way you only use your magic for the spell."

"Do you think there wasn't enough fairy magic?" He couldn't use all his magic. Fernlight knew that. He would fade and have to restore himself for a whole day.

"I don't, but something got in the way." She lifted a string from the box.

"Wait," Bramble said. He flew through the door and settled on his desktop. He had emergency treasure. The fairy magic soaked into the gold and jewels would save him from exhaustion. He looked around the room. No one paid any attention. Only a few brownies were lurking under Lionel's desk. Pit still stared at the screen like he could force information to make sense. You never knew if a brownie was paying attention, but Bramble decided the risk was worth it. If the treasure magic worked to show Agnes the killer, they would be free of observation.

He thought the spell to open the sealed drawer. Before slipping a hand in to pull out the ten pieces of treasure, Bramble looked for spies again. Still no one watching. He zipped his hand inside and pulled out the rubies, thinking the sealing spell and putting the jewels inside his pocket so fast no one would know.

When he returned to the workroom, Fernlight was walking the circle and letting the string slide through her fingers. None of them had been able to toss it in the air to form the circle as it fell like Heath had done.

Agnes sat on the exposed earth, the ingredients laid out in the center.

"Time to solve the case," Bramble said, slipping inside to land beside Agnes. "Do you need to ask questions?"

Fernlight closed the circle and Agnes shook her head. Not like she was saying no, but like something was inside.

"What's wrong?" he asked.

"Pressure. My ears plug when the protections are active. It doesn't hurt. I'll keep my questions until after you are done."

Bramble pulled one of the shoes from the box. "We will save the other one in case we have to show the judge and lawyer the spell. See how I am learning?"

Agnes smiled, but didn't speak.

Bramble finished his preparations, then activated the spell. This time they saw the scene from a different angle. Like the shoes were watching the action. Now the killer came up to the victim's waist when he hung up on the beam. The shoes couldn't see the face, and the clothes the killer wore were very bulky. Why didn't the spell show them how the body got up there? It started too late to help anyone learn what happened. Was he dead first? Was he killed in the building?

The body jerked and bumped the killer away. "See that?" Bramble asked. "We can identify his jaw."

The killer bent to pick up something below what the shoes would see, then turned away as he tossed blood on the wall from a bucket.

Bramble dodged before he remembered it wasn't real.

Then the vision blurred and faded away.

"It's not enough," Fernlight said.

Bramble rubbed the rubies in his pocket. There was still magic and there shouldn't be. The only magic used by the spell was his. Something blocked the power. Fernlight knew better, which meant only one culprit.

"Agnes, what have you brought into the circle?" he asked.

She touched her chest. "Only jewelry."

"We need to look at it," Fernlight said, holding up a hand to stop him flying to grab whatever was under her shirt.

She lifted a chain to show a pendant.

"Bringing magic into the circle is dangerous," Bramble whispered. Too much protection was worse than too little.

"It's not magic," Agnes said. "This has been in my family for generations."

Bramble reached for the pendant, but he couldn't get close. "It is a protection spell. I don't know who made it." *Is Agnes like Dionne? A hidden magical person?*

"We can research how you came to own this later," Fernlight said. "We need you to place it outside the circle, Agnes. If Bramble has enough magic left, we can try again when it's gone."

Agnes closed her hand around the pendant.

She is worried that we can't protect her or won't!

"You will be safe," he said. "I promise. Your magic just needs to go on the other side of the salt."

Agnes took in a big breath and then nodded. Fernlight opened the ends of the salt circle and muttered a spell to keep them safe. Agnes tossed the silver amulet and chain outside and Fernlight re-twisted the string.

As soon as the circle was complete again, Bramble felt the power from the rubies flow into him.

He rushed to activate the spell again. At least they hadn't burned the sage, so no need to go retrieve more.

This time the details were clear. They saw the wrinkles in the killer's clothes and the tiny jerks of the body. What didn't change was the angle. Nothing more than the glimpse of a jaw.

He lit the sage and released the spell. Fernlight cleaned up the remnants of the ingredients.

"Bramble, you look faded," Agnes said as she bent and put the chain around her neck.

"One hour of sleep will help," he said. "I will need to get more of the secret ingredient." His wife would not be pleased to relinquish more of their treasure. "I hoped we would recognize the killer and we could arrest him. Then this case would be over."

"Sorry, Bramble, that's not how it works. You will need to prove the magic didn't just fill in a face or the case will fail."

Too many rules!

CHAPTER THIRTY-SEVEN

Their first interview was with a hot dog vendor in the business district. Lionel tried to dredge up some optimism that the minister would have blurted out a whole story of threats and kidnappings with some man who sold lunches.

"Why are we starting here?" he asked Rhodri. "Do we know what time the contact happened?"

Rhodri dodged a crowd of tourists who were looking at phones and holding them up as they turned in circles. "The kids put the contacts in order by the images they saw. The time of day by the light and the flow of people, and they explained a lot of other indicators that involved the scent of the closest flowers. I couldn't follow the fairy logic."

"They didn't find anything to indicate what happened? Like an image of someone grabbing the minister?" Lionel laughed, and then wondered if it was possible in the future to do just that.

"I thought starting at the beginning would be best," Rhodri said. They were crossing a busy intersection on the way to the art gallery. "There may be a clue earlier that will allow us to jump ahead, but if not, we'll understand better how he lived his life."

Another search through too much data.

"If he had lived, Heath would be rich and important," Lionel said. "I think there must be a way to look at a lot of seemingly unrelated information to highlight the important pieces. Maybe when I get to move in and we've sorted his spells out, I can continue his work."

"Maybe put that off until we catch the murderer," Rhodri said. "Why are you moving into Heath's house?"

Lionel explained how they had released the lock on the spell book, and what Pit was doing with the information. "It would be faster if he didn't need to enter everything in a spreadsheet before we even find out if it can be organized."

"Our hot dog vendor is on the corner," Rhodri said, pointing to a cart at the intersection ahead. "Shade is meeting us here. She didn't like the idea of riding on my shoulder through downtown."

"No, I did not," Shade piped up from the window ledge of the store behind them.

"How long have you been there?" Lionel asked. He appreciated the sneakiness more when someone else was the target.

"Before you got here," she said. "What do you want me to do?"

"Sneak around while we ask questions," Lionel said. "That goes for all the interviews today. You'll see things we can't."

Shade leaned against the window and crossed her arms. "We no longer like the word, sneak. Please use something else. Like infiltrate, like reconnoiter, maybe scout. These words do not make us sound untrustworthy."

"Surveillance is probably the best in this case," Lionel said. Bramble's distrust of brownies had infected his language. Although Bramble often seemed proud to be sneaky.

"Shouldn't we ask Agnes if this is acceptable?" Rhodri asked.

"No," Shade said before Lionel could answer. "This is brownie business, and we will not explain our methods."

Lionel looked around. No one noticed they were talking to a tiny dust-covered being. "Kim said that the police often do the same thing," he said. "They look around for things in plain sight that they can use to solve a case."

"In plain sight for a brownie is very different from what a human might think," Rhodri said. "And if she finds anything, Shade may be called to court as a witness."

"Then they must find a way for someone my size to give testimony," Shade said. "I am not afraid of it. I have researched many stories about being a witness."

Stories are not the same as real life.

"Are we ready?" Lionel looked toward the vendor. "He's not busy now, but I don't want to stand in line when he has customers."

They agreed to meet at the same location after the interview.

Lionel let Rhodri lead the way to the man standing behind the grill that was giving off the enticing aroma of grilled onions.

"May we ask you a few questions?" Rhodri asked. "We are private investigators, and we think you may have information to help us with a case."

The man looked them over and flipped a stack of onions. "I don't know anything about a case."

"My name is Rhodri, and this man is Lionel." Rhodri waited for a name, but the man just looked back.

"You don't want to get involved," Lionel said. "I under-stand that. We want some information. We'll forget where we got it as soon as we leave." One of the steps in the manual for private investigators he'd found online listed steps to an interview. Put the target at ease was number one. Although thinking of people as targets didn't feel like it put anyone at ease.

"What do you want? My customers will come soon."

Lionel pulled out a small notebook to pretend he was taking notes. Another step from the manual.

Rhodri explained who they were looking for and said the minister had lost something that day. He didn't say he'd lost himself.

"Yeah, he comes a few times a month," the vendor said. "Likes extra onions. Says his wife wants him to eat healthy, but he needs something tasty. I told him to tell her onions are a vegetable."

"Anything odd the last time he came?" Rhodri asked.

Lionel pretended to take notes while he listened and tried to catch Shade on her mission. Not a glimpse of her.

"No. He was on his way to a meeting. He's always on his way to a meeting. I guess that's what politicians do."

Time to move on.

"Did he say who he was meeting?" Rhodri kept the interview going to Lionel's surprise.

"Some corporate big wig," the vendor answered. Then he pushed the onions to the side and pulled out a container of hot dogs. "That's all I can tell you. Now it's lunch time and I need to make a living."

Lionel led the way to the meeting point. "I hope Shade found something."

"I did not," she announced. "It is better when the interview is in a place where there are things."

CHAPTER THIRTY-EIGHT

Bramble woke after exactly one hour. The rest helped, but tonight he would face his wife and exchange the rubies for fresh treasure.

"Did I miss anything?" he asked, floating toward where Fernlight stood behind Kim at the computer.

"Not yet," Kim said. "We've been trying to find information on all the names we have. Yours from the spell, and Pit's from researching that company."

"Where is Agnes?" If she was gone for the day, there were so many things Bramble could do without having to explain.

"She went in search of coffee," Fernlight said.

"Should be back soon," Kim added. "Why?"

Kim was too smart for him to hide anything from her. "What if we made a circle and asked it to show us each of the names?"

Fernlight straightened up and rubbed her eyelids. "That screen is hard to look at for long periods," she said. "You mean the spell we did to find Talbot Ryce?"

Bramble's wings started to tremble at the memory of that spell. When the image of the human had spoken directly to

Heath and wouldn't leave when commanded. "Without the scary part, yes."

Kim printed out some information from the computer. "We have some images here," she said, collecting the papers. "Searching through social media and other mentions online is taking forever. Tell me what you plan."

If Agnes was coming back soon, Bramble would have to explain twice.

The door to the inner office opened and Agnes nudged it wide with her hips. "Coffee as ordered," she said. "I couldn't resist some of these cookies."

Bramble didn't want any of the treats. "We have a plan."

Agnes handed Kim one of the cups and placed the bag of cookies on a desk. "Magic?"

"Of course."

She waited for an explanation.

Fernlight explained how the spell would work. She didn't mention the frightening possibility someone would know they were watching. That was only possible for Talbot Ryce because he took the magic drug. No one else would be able to take control.

"I'd love to see that," Kim said. "Can we all fit in the circle?"

It would be too crowded to fit in all the images. "Our room is too small to create a large enough protection for all of us," Fernlight said. "Bramble can do the magic, but he will be the only one able to do the spell if I stay outside."

"Can you cast in the lobby?" Agnes asked. "It's twice the size of the workroom. Then we will all fit. I don't want Bramble to take too many risks."

"I am brave enough to handle it," Bramble said. *Where had those words come from? He was not brave enough.*

"If we cast in the lobby, we will need to seal the office," Fernlight said. "That means Lionel, Rhodri, Leith, and Raj will not be able to enter. Or any of the brownies if they are still outside."

"I'm sure I'll get another chance," Kim said. "I'll wait out here."

Fernlight looked at Kim and then Agnes. She was thinking, and Bramble had an awful feeling he wasn't going to like the result.

"I know the spell," she finally said. "There is little risk. Having you inside, Kim, would be useful because you may observe something as an investigator and a human that we would not. I will stay out here and wait for you to tell me what you find."

"I will also be inside," Pit said.

How do I keep forgetting he's here?

"What special skill would you bring?" Bramble asked. "Everyone must have a purpose. Kim is a trained investigator. Agnes needs to observe. I must control the magic."

Pit walked to the edge of the desk and stood with his hands on his hips. "Brownies see things. We do not take up room. You can't stop me anyway."

"I can stop you." Bramble let his wings carry him to the desk. "When the string is sealed, you cannot enter."

Pit just smiled and raised an eyebrow.

"Fine!" Bramble said, deciding the only way to win an argument with Pit was to refuse to start one. "You must be quiet, and do not spy on fairy magic."

Pit climbed down the desk and disappeared underneath.

Bramble flew to the spell room door and opened it while carefully watching the floor. No sign of Pit entering.

"Come on," he called to Kim and Agnes. "We should do it now. And please leave your amulet outside, Agnes."

. . .

The spell was starting to work. Little bubbles showing the people popped into existence. Bramble waited until they had one for every name before preparing the next step.

"Kim and Pit, you can check if the paper image is the same as the one in the bubble," he said. "If they are not, then the bubble is the right image."

He saw all three of his observers bend over the printouts. Kim put a check mark next to each picture. There was no discrepancy. Good.

"In the first test, we only asked for images," he said. "We didn't get a chance to see what the people were doing." He stopped speaking before he told them why.

"This time you are going to show us videos?" Agnes asked. "Surveillance?"

Bramble looked at Kim; she shrugged. "I guess like drones? They are flying devices that can record people without their knowledge or consent."

That is very rude. Humans are full of contradictions. If they want privacy, why do they invent invisible cameras?

"No. And yes, I suppose." He pulled his thoughts together. This was not where he expected to explain simple things. "The magic is watching and making movies of what it sees. The movies will only be here."

Pit sat on the ground beside Kim. "So, you want to watch the people to make a decision if they are good or bad?"

"Yes," Bramble said, surprised Pit understood. "But only if they are people who might be the killer."

"I'm not sure you can make the determination that way," Agnes said, "but let's see."

Bramble made Pit look down at the ground while he cast the spell.

CHAPTER THIRTY-NINE

The bubbles stopped multiplying after only a few moments. Bramble flew around and peeked at each image to make sure no one was paying attention to him. They were safe.

"So how do we eliminate them?" Kim asked. "Solid police work requires more than just looking at one quick scenario to decide who is innocent and who is guilty."

Pit and Agnes stared at him too. They all wanted the answer. He was the only one smart enough to know. *So much for brownies and their special skills.*

"We cannot be sure," he said as he floated down to the ground. This time he needed to think like a druid. Teaching was important. "We first look for something that is not quite right. Then we watch for a while to see if we can figure out what is going on. We dismiss the bubbles we think are less important."

"Why are some of them just colored circles?" Pit asked. "Are they what we mean as not right?"

Two of the bubbles showed only flat red circles. Bramble was going to talk about them next. Pit should have waited. "Those people are sleeping or dead or something," he said.

"We will figure out what later. It is important to look at the information in front of us, not guess too soon."

"How do we know who they are?" Kim asked. "I mean, the ones in the images we couldn't find before."

Bramble turned to look up at the circling images. "Oh." He clicked his fingers and names appeared. "I forgot that part."

Agnes was writing in her notebook and not looking at him any longer. Good, he wasn't interested in teaching her. He only wanted to teach investigators.

"Can I walk around them?" Kim asked. "It's a bit hard on my neck to keep looking up."

"I will sit on your shoulder," Pit said. "I will see more from there."

The bubbles would only go when he dismissed them, so walking around wouldn't destroy any of the videos. But what if Kim accidentally moved the salt string? "Will you be very, very, very careful? If you trip over the string, the circle will break, and I don't have enough energy to redo this. We will need to wait a whole day."

Kim glanced around the string. "The circle is pretty small. Can we call a bubble to us? That way we stay safely here and still get to look at the details."

Bramble looked at the bubbles. All had names attached. "Yes. That will work. We should each look at the same one, not call who we want."

He walked across the circle to join them. They decided to call Dominic Stenmark. He was Ivan's cousin.

The bubble showed a man with black hair and a beard. He was running, but Bramble couldn't see anyone chasing him.

"Jogging doesn't tell us much," Kim said. "But if he's running away from someone, it might be a clue."

Bramble moved a little closer to the bubble to try to catch any tiny details.

"Humans run for exercise," Pit said. "I think this man is not involved. He is not running near this city. There are no mountains and there is no storm here."

Waves crashed against the wall beside Dominic. Pit was right, and Bramble wished each bubble would be so easy to understand. "Shall I dismiss it?"

Now Agnes paid attention. "What if we need to look at it again? Not this video. I agree with Pit; this is not anywhere near Vancouver. But enough time has passed since the killing that this cousin could have committed the murder and gone somewhere across the world."

"Until we break the circle, I can recall the bubble. If we really need to look at it after that, we will need to recreate the circle and it will not be this again unless he runs all the time."

"That's good for the people who'll be upset about violating privacy, but not so great when it comes to presenting evidence." Agnes pointed to one of the other bubbles. "Can we look at that one next?"

Bramble ignored her comments about privacy. If the man runs on a public street, how can he expect to keep it private?

He called the Vivianne Braithwaite bubble over.

"Why is it fuzzy?" Kim asked.

"Yes, is there something wrong with the magic?" Pit asked.

"Nothing is wrong with my magic!" Bramble moved the bubble closer to him. It was fuzzy, like someone put a thin curtain up. "We should try to look at her in real life," he said. "I think someone gave her protection. Why is she on this list of names?"

"She came up when you asked for the names of people who knew him," Agnes said.

Kim squinted at the bubble. "She's at work somewhere. I

can't see what she's doing, but definitely some kind of paper-work. That looks like a home office."

"We will try to find her," Pit said.

Bramble dismissed the bubble, and they continued to look at and discard all the bubbles until they got to the two that were red. Bramble closed his eyes and pushed more magic at the people. When he opened his eyes, nothing changed. "I cannot make it work," he said, embarrassed to admit it in front of Pit and Agnes. Kim wouldn't mind; she knew sometimes magic didn't work.

"We didn't have a chance to screen these before coming in," Kim said. "I'll check the hospitals and morgues when we finish."

"It was a good plan," Pit said. "We have some people to visit. I will wait until Kim finishes her screening, and then my horde and I will start investigating the people."

Bramble noticed Agnes wince. Good, she didn't trust brownies either!

"We should take the time for that talk, Pit," Agnes said, "before anyone goes on surveillance. I need to learn a little more about your methods."

CHAPTER FORTY

This didn't seem like a good way to spend time, Bramble thought. They had nothing new and no clear suspects, and now he didn't know what to do.

"Before we finish," Agnes said. "I would like to understand how recalling the videos works. Can you bring back the most active ones?"

Bramble concentrated, and four bubbles appeared again. He didn't understand what she meant about active, but these were the ones they had looked at most.

"It would be nice to hear what they are saying," Agnes said. "Obviously, I don't really know what an investigator needs, but more is always better, right?"

Bramble looked at her. He noticed Pit doing the same.

"Yes, maybe next time?" Kim said.

"There is sound," Pit said.

"I don't hear anything," Kim said. Agnes shook her head too.

Pit looked up at him. "You forgot to take it out of fairy and brownie range."

Bramble didn't answer, he was so mad at himself. It was

bad enough to forget, but to give a brownie a chance to point out his mistake was unforgivable. He concentrated again and the bubbles filled with murmuring voices.

"Here," he said, bringing one bubble out of the crowd. "You should be able to listen to what is going on. Not just voices, but the sounds around them.

Kim started making notes. "Did you hear anything interesting from any of the other bubbles?"

"Is that what you meant by most active?" Bramble asked.

She looked up from her notebook. "Let's start again," she said. "Not all the bubbles. Think about what you heard, you and Pit. Then eliminate all the ones who were talking about innocent things."

"How do we know what is innocent?" Pit asked.

"If they are talking to children," Agnes said, "or about entertainment. Or a sport. We can probably leave them until we run out of ideas."

Pit told Bramble the names he thought were interesting enough to recall. He talked in the fairy range, so Bramble didn't need to feel any more angry or embarrassed. He added two more names, and then three of the existing bubbles disappeared and two new ones took their place.

"Grant Norman, Anne Rivers, Vivianne Braithwaite, and James Connor." Kim wrote the names on pages in her notebook. "Okay, let's start with Mr. Norman."

Bramble swooped the bubble down to float in front of Kim. He watched as she wrote notes.

Mr. Norman at a desk - can we get a location? Reading a paper report. He is commenting, and we see him taking notes. There is nothing in the video or audio to suggest criminal activity.

"Anyone think we should be worried about him?" she asked.

"Seems like he's doing business," Pit said. "We see this kind of thing all the time. If we can find out where his office is, some of my horde can look closer." He turned to look directly at Agnes. "Yes, after you have talked about our methods and tried to steal brownie secrets."

Agnes just smiled at him.

"Next," Kim said.

Bramble floated Anne Rivers' bubble to Kim.

Ms. Rivers appears to be teaching a kindergarten class. Unlikely to be in a position to drive the actions needed to kill Ivan (or kidnap a minister).

Bramble noticed that the Braithwaite bubble was empty, so he brought James Connor's in next.

Mr. Connor is in an office talking to an off-screen subject. He is speaking Portuguese, and the time on his phone indicates he is in time zone GMT-3, which includes Brazil. Unlikely to be involved in any of the cases.

"What does that mean?" Agnes asked. "He's unlikely to be involved? Do you discard them as suspects?"

Kim nodded for Bramble to bring the last bubble down. "No, we do need to look a little further into them, like Annie River, who could be connected to someone who might have committed the murder or the kidnapping, and even psychopaths can put on a friendly face. But our main effort will be elsewhere. Remember, some of these people will be his friends, and some will only know him slightly."

The Vivianne woman was back in the bubble. She was at a desk too, in an office. She was looking up at someone and giving orders. "I don't care about your excuses; get the job done, and don't come back until you've cleaned up your mess. If you can't do that, maybe you'll understand what it's like to be on the receiving end."

Bramble looked at Kim's notebook.

Ms. Braithwaite. Aggressive behavior toward unknown subject.

"She has the attitude," Kim said. "We should find out

what this job is. Maybe nothing, but this is the most promising we have."

Bramble cleared out the bubbles while thinking of spells that might help them find more answers on these people.

"I suppose I will speak with you when we leave the circle," Pit said to Agnes. "My horde has a lot of investigating to do."

Bramble broke the circle and opened the door to the office. Pit was not going to take all the interesting jobs away. He would talk to Fernlight about the way brownies should fit within the team. He wished they weren't so useful, but that battle was lost.

CHAPTER FORTY-ONE

The feud between Bramble and Pit was not her business. Agnes's heart drew her to help them make peace, but her brain understood the animosity was based on a much deeper and cultural base than just what she saw. And her help was as likely to make it worse than heal the rift.

She drew Pit aside as soon as they were in the office. "Let's talk now about your methods."

"I do not understand your laws," Pit said. "Brownies always go where they wish."

"Probably best not to advertise that," she said. No one understood the ramifications of magic in their lives. Most people worried about what it meant now. Very few dug into the past and looked at what magic might have influenced.

"What do you want me to say?" Pit asked. "It is important that we start observing this woman. You are holding things up."

There was no rancor in his voice. Pit simply stated facts. It was refreshing sometimes to work with people who had no hidden agenda. "How do you get into places? How are people giving you permission? I think for now, that will do. We'll dig into more detail later if we need to."

"I cannot say how we enter places. If our way is not the same way as everyone, it is a brownie secret." The arms-crossed stance made it obvious he wouldn't tell.

"It is important to know how you obtain permission." Agnes would not be so easily dismissed. This was important. Without authorization to use magic, this team would be no different from a human investigation agency.

Pit closed his eyes and muttered something she couldn't catch. Then he looked up and said, "This is a brownie secret, but I think we can safely tell people. We cannot enter any place without permission."

That will need to be proved. "I believe you, Pit. But others will not. Can you explain more?"

"No. We can prove it," he said. "I think so anyway. If we are told not to go somewhere and then we try and fail, would that be enough?"

With a bit of finessing. "Send one of your horde out of hearing. I will tell you where brownies cannot enter. Then call the individual back, and we will run the test. It will suffice for me."

"Dust," Pit called. A brownie streaked in grit ran out from under Lionel's desk. "Go to where you cannot hear us and return in one minute."

Dust scurried back toward their secret exit under the desk.

"Pick your place," Pit said.

There were a variety of places in the office for Agnes to pick. She wanted to be able to see the results, so her choice needed to be in the open. "The chair in the corner. He is not allowed to pass underneath."

They waited the few seconds for Dust to appear. The

brownie didn't know anything about the experiment, or even that it existed.

"Go and wait under that chair for instructions," Pit said.

Dust turned on his heel and marched toward the chair. As he took the step to pass under the edge, blue light flashed, and he bounced off an invisible barrier onto his back.

Bramble laughed and pointed out the poor brownie on the floor. "Do it again!"

Pit glared at Bramble and told Dust to return to the horde. "Good enough?"

Agnes tried to dredge up some doubt, but it was clear Dust wasn't pretending. "That will do for now," she said. "At some point, you will need to explain how you get permission, but not now." She returned to her report.

"Please remove the restriction," Pit said. "We must be able to move freely."

Agnes said the words to remove the barrier.

"We have a plan," Bramble called to Agnes, "before the brownies go spying."

"We can get a bit more of her surroundings in this," Fernlight said, pointing to a small globe on the desk. "It will give the brownies some guidance."

Agnes peered at the ball. Vivianne Braithwaite's home office. She was alone now and fiddling with something on her desk. This kind of surveillance still needed to be regulated, but was it different from bugging an office? The only issue Agnes could think of was speed. A warrant to bug a location often took days to enact because bugs needed to be put in place. This magical observation happened right away. Only a benefit.

"Be careful what you do with the information you find this way," she warned.

As Agnes spoke, she observed Vivianne tap her desk twice and then lift the top. Inside was a small compartment holding five objects, one of which looked exactly like the string Bramble used to create the circle of protection.

"Magic objects," Bramble announced. "It's her. That's one of Heath's inventions. We should arrest her and make her talk."

"We can't arrest people," Fernlight said.

Agnes was thankful they had a check in place for that. "You can't just assume these objects tie her to the cases."

"But she has Heath's string," Bramble said.

"And it is possible she bought the items from him," Agnes said. "And those other things might be just as innocent. Even if she's implicated, you still have the murder and the minister's disappearance to solve."

"Jumping in without thinking will give her a chance to run," Kim said, joining them to look at the image. "It's a good spell because we're pointed in a direction. But Pit needs to do his job now. Your spell gave them something to work on."

Agnes watched as Vivianne reached out to stroke one of the amulets in the drawer; avarice seemed to glow around her. She knew from her cases that people who collected possibly illicit items often had that same feeling.

CHAPTER FORTY-TWO

After five unproductive interviews, Lionel began to despair of finding anything to lead them to the minister. "It's like he just wandered through the day. People remember him and like him, but there's nothing beyond the superficial."

Rhodri looked around for Shade. "It will only take one," he said. "We only have a few names left. At least we'll be sure we finished investigating this lead."

They were waiting for Shade to return from scouting the last interview, a librarian. The building was huge for one brownie to search, but she'd set off with a look of joy on her face.

"I am finished."

Lionel looked down, and Shade looked back from her seat on his shoe. "I think I want to go to all the libraries. Pit will be very excited to learn how much we have to search. I wonder why we haven't been in one before."

When the case was over, the brownies could snoop to their heart's content. "The next one is two blocks away. An office building," Lionel said. "Do you know the office number?"

She started climbing his pant leg. "Yes. But I hate elevators, and the stairs are too high for me without the help of the horde. I will come in your pocket."

Lionel clapped his hand over the opening to his jacket pocket. Too many charms to be safe for a brownie. "Jeans pocket."

"Oh, look, a tiny one just for a brownie. Why did the humans make a pocket like this if they didn't know about brownies?"

"I'm sure they designed it for a different use," Rhodri said. "How will we know you are ready to leave? What if we need to go before you are done?"

Lionel looked down at the tiny dusty-haired head sticking out under his belt. Shade was safely snuggled in.

"Druids are very smart. If I finish first, I will pinch Lionel's ankle. Then I'll climb in here again. If you must leave first, wait for me in the hall outside."

The walk to the building and elevator ride took only minutes. There was a hall outside the office of Norman Consulting, so no problem waiting for Shade if needed.

She wiggled out of his pocket and rode his jeans to the floor. Lionel tried the door, unlocked. He stepped through, but even though he knew she was with them, he did not see Shade slip in.

The office was an open design. A desk that Lionel guessed formed some sort of reception area stood empty. In the far corner, at a large desk, sat the man they were looking for, Grant Norman.

"Can I help you?" he called as he started walking toward them.

Lionel let Rhodri take the lead. In the interviews up to now, Rhodri asked a set of standard questions. Lionel would pretend to take notes, but really, he created questions specific to the subject. It had worked in the way that more information came out from their subject, but not always useful information, unfortunately.

Rhodri explained their reason for coming. Grant Norman offered them coffee or tea, and they declined. He invited them to sit at his desk and sat back, waiting.

"When you met with the minister, did you notice anything different about him?"

Grant tipped his head to the side, thinking. "No, just his usual friendly self."

"Did he say where he was going next?" Rhodri asked.

"Usually, he would be going back to his office, but perhaps not that day?"

"You said his usual friendly self," Rhodri continued. "How often would he visit?"

Grant leaned forward as if sharing a confidence. "He would come by for his order twice a month."

Order? Lionel looked around the room. There were cupboards that might contain inventory, but nothing indicating the kind of business he did. Shade would know but asking the question might be interesting. "What order? I thought a consulting business sold their services."

Grant's smile grew. Lionel didn't buy it; this was simply a pose that he found useful.

"We do provide services, but we also facilitate the purchase of products. Nothing illegal, just a little difficult to get without the right contacts."

"What products exactly did the minister buy?" Rhodri asked.

"I'm not sure I should share that information. The minister did ask for confidentiality."

"We are working for the family," Rhodri said, not quite a lie. "Would Mrs. Chan be aware of these products?"

"Possibly," Grant admitted. "If I can rely on your discretion? They were cultural artifacts and some natural medicine ingredients. Nothing illegal, as I said."

Lionel felt Shade's pinch and then saw her climb over his knee on her way to the pocket. "Can we see the records of these items?" *Why is the man stalling?*

"Perhaps that is a step too far," Grant said. Then he stood. "I must prepare for my next meeting."

"Would the products have anything to do with Feng Shui?" Rhodri asked.

An emotion flickered in Grant's eyes. Fear? Anger?

"Some, yes."

"If you think of anything else you can tell us," Rhodri said, "you can reach us here." He handed Grant a business card.

Grant escorted them to the door and closed it behind them.

Lionel checked his pocket. Shade grinned up at him.

"We should talk on the street," Rhodri said. "I have a feeling he's listening."

On the street, Shade hopped out of her pocket and onto a concrete plant holder. "I didn't find anything that said he was hiding the minister, but it is not only medicine and beads. He had magical objects in his office recently. I think he meant not illegal because no one has made laws about magical objects yet."

"He's definitely hiding something," Rhodri said. "He's a good candidate for brownie surveillance."

"I will tell Pit when we are done," Shade said.

"The next person is across the city," Rhodri said. "Do you have the phone? We can call her before we head through the magical paths."

Lionel listened to a fast one-sided conversation. Whoever was on the other end set up an appointment for the next day.

"We're not getting anywhere," Lionel said. "The last one on our list is a coffee shop owner. He'll give us the same story as everyone else."

"I agree," Rhodri said. "I think it's time to talk to the family. I'm curious why they haven't been in contact."

CHAPTER FORTY-THREE

The minister's family lived in a quiet area filled with large homes that filled the lot, leaving no green space in front other than a strip of grass that bordered the road. The setting gave off an unwelcoming feeling. At least for a magical being, no grass, flowers, or trees created an unsettling atmosphere, and there was no environment for local fairies and sprites so the plants didn't thrive as they should.

"I will be outside when you are finished," Shade said, pointing to the curb. She disappeared.

"We should handle this differently," Rhodri said. "It's not an interrogation, but we still need to get what we can from them."

"A wife and two kids," Lionel said. "Kids are probably in school. I think we still start with you asking the questions. It occurred to me that if the family isn't the reason he's disappeared, we might find another fake good luck charm."

"Just go gently," Rhodri said.

They rang the doorbell and waited. The door was heavy wood with a small, tinted window placed at head height so Lionel couldn't see anything inside.

He was about ready to ring the bell again when the door opened. A woman in her mid-forties, by the look of her, stared back. Black hair in a ponytail, no makeup, jeans, and an old tee-shirt, she didn't show any signs of worry about her husband.

Rhodri introduced them and asked if she was Mrs. Chan.

"Yes. Come in. I don't have a contact number for my husband, but I'm happy to answer any questions."

They followed her into the kitchen and sat at the small table, looking out over a large, well-landscaped garden, enough to almost make up for the lack of green space in the front. Again refusing refreshments, Rhodri asked, "When you say you don't have a contact number, where is your husband?"

Lionel listened while he cast his senses out. Definitely something wrong in the house.

"He's at a conference in Barcelona," she said. "Something to do with magical accords. He left a couple of days ago."

"And he hasn't reached out since?"

"No. That's not unusual. He works hard, and I prefer him to get his rest."

It felt like someone was watching him. Lionel resisted the urge to go searching for the source. Shade knew her job. If there was something or someone to find, she would find it.

He glanced along the baseboards hoping to see the brownie as she moved around the house but didn't catch even a glimpse of her. *Well, she can always come back with help if we need her to.*

"Has anything odd happened in the last few days?" Rhodri asked. "Perhaps a gift?"

So, he could feel it too. Their job wasn't to tell the woman her husband had gone missing, but not doing so hampered the questioning process. And perhaps she was just hiding the fact that she'd done something to him. The internet was full of stories of spouses disposing of each other.

"When my husband took the portfolio, we decided not to accept anything from magical folk since we didn't understand what the implications might be."

"And from non-magical sources?" Rhodri asked.

"Not that I've accepted." She looked around her. "The kids might have. I can ask them tonight."

"Thank you, Mrs. Chan." Rhodri gave her his card. "Anything you think of, just call."

"You can call me Mae," she said. "This isn't about my husband being at a conference, right?"

Lionel stopped trying to find the source of the feeling and turned his attention to Mae. She stared at Rhodri and held the card in her fingers.

"You are private investigators. You're trying to get dirt on Connor."

Rhodri pointed to the card. "We are not the usual kind of investigators. I am a druid; Lionel is a wizard. We are not here to cause trouble or to gather anything but information."

Mae relaxed a little, but the suspicion still lurked. "Yeah, but you haven't been up front about the information you want. If you don't tell me right now, I'll call the cops."

Lionel touched Rhodri's arm. A barrier stood between Mae and the druid now. It was almost visible. She wasn't ready to hear the truth from him.

"I'm sorry we are the ones to bring you this news," Lionel said. "Your husband is not in Barcelona."

She shot up. "Where is he? They warned us something might happen if he got involved with you people."

As she yelled, Lionel felt a surge of the sense that someone was watching again. Something here was causing agitation. He reached into his pocket and broke a calming charm. It only took the edge off her anger but did give him a chance to reach her.

"We don't know where your husband is. Queen Maeve is

concerned and asked that we find him." He pressed the charm a little harder and Mae regained her seat.

"When? Am I in danger? My kids?"

"A little more than two days ago. We are following his last steps to find a clue. Did he say anything in the last few days that would cause you concern?"

Rhodri smoothed a sheet of paper on the table. Lionel recognized the spell and hoped he would find the source of the interference.

"No. Everything is fine." She noticed Rhodri. "What are you doing?"

He looked up from the paper. "Something in your house is causing mayhem. I am trying to find it."

"I told you there is nothing," she snapped, her temper starting to rise again.

"I assure you something is causing problems," Lionel said. "Please ask your children if they received any gifts. Do you have a housekeeper?"

"I'll ask her and let you know."

Relieved that his calmness minimized the effect of whatever had contaminated this home, he asked Rhodri, "Anything?"

"No, this thing is well hidden. Mrs. Chan, we may need to send a bigger search team. Will you accept a protection charm in the meantime? It will not completely cancel out the problem but will make the effect manageable."

"Maybe we should move out," Mae said. "I'll take your charm anyway."

Rhodri folded the paper and placed it back in his pocket. Lionel handed Mae a walnut holding the protection, giving it a rub as he did. "Just set this somewhere, as the magic works passively.

"It is not a good idea to move out of the house. You will alert whoever planted this thing and they may escalate their activities. I will ask your garden fairies and sprites to keep an eye out. They are very effective."

When they were on the street again, Shade scurried across the concrete sidewalk and climbed Lionel's leg.

"It is too big for me to search properly. Not like the library, but because that spell is making me confused. I don't know where this bad thing is because it's all over the house."

"You can come back with the horde," Lionel said. "She didn't say no."

"Good. No spell is powerful enough to confuse a horde."

CHAPTER FORTY-FOUR

Bramble needed to leave soon. His strength was almost gone, and he needed some to be able to tell Thorn why she should give him more treasure and not make him wait until he rested enough to restore his magic the normal way.

Agnes had left them and would be gone until morning. The freedom to act without explaining helped him think. Everyone except Raj and Leith were back in the office trying to make sense of what they'd found. Lionel had just asked the horde to all go to the minister's family's house to find the source of the bad feeling.

"Raj is calling," Fernlight said before she put the phone on speaker setting so they could all hear.

"Hello, Raj," Bramble shouted to the phone. "Have you found us some clues?"

Raj chuckled and said goodbye to someone on his end. He was still in the HOP-D office.

"Listen, we did find something," Raj said. "Can we meet somewhere to talk? I don't want to wait until I get to the office."

"You can tell us now," Lionel said. "We're all here."

Raj didn't answer right away. After a moment, he said, "I need to tell you in person, not the kind of thing you talk about on the phone."

"Leith can create a circle," Fernlight said. "We'll be able to see you."

"He's gone to update Maeve, so she won't need to interrupt us. Is there somewhere we can meet? A restaurant. I missed lunch."

"Banks'," Bramble shouted. "It is a perfect place, and we can tell Leith and he can join us."

"The magic pub? No one can find it. Oh, I guess you can. How do I get to it?"

Bramble told Raj the exact directions and how to recognize the door, which was under a glamor, and to tell Mark he was meeting Bramble when he arrived. "How long?"

"No more than a half hour," Raj said, then he ended the call.

"I will go," Bramble said. "I can collect the information and come back much faster than any of you."

"Not faster than us," Briar said. His sister, Thistle, nodded.

"You are not investigators yet." It might be too dangerous. And if Bramble asked for treasure and had to tell Thorn that he'd let the kids be hurt, she would never let him come back.

"It shouldn't only be one of us," Lionel said. "We should be careful now that we've found a few clues. We can't even find what's creating disruption in the minister's home. That should tell us we're not infallible. I'll go with Bramble."

"Perhaps we should all go," Kim said. "I kind of miss Mark's stew."

"No! I am not afraid to go alone."

Fernlight held up her hands and patted the air. "We cannot drop everything and all go to Banks'. Someone needs to be here if the brownies come back. You all have research to do that might point us in the direction of the minister or of the murderer."

"Who then?" Rhodri asked. "I am happy to stay here and research. I may be able to suggest a contact at the grove to allow my fellow druids to assist—if I know the actual questions."

Bramble didn't trust himself to speak. He was too depleted to spend energy in thinking up arguments.

"I'll go with Lionel and Bramble," Fernlight said. "We'll bring Raj back with us. I'll make sure we leave a message for Leith to return."

"We should go now," Bramble said. "It would be better if we arrived first because Raj won't know how to act or who to talk to."

"One more thing," Fernlight said as she pulled on her jacket. "You will go to your tribe and rest afterward. I don't want you fading away when we need you to act with us."

"I just need to talk to Thorn. I can come right back." He wasn't going to sleep while everyone solved the cases.

"Say hello to Mother," Thistle said.

"You can do that yourself," Bramble said. "It's late and we can work without you until tomorrow."

"But..." Briar must have seen the stern look Bramble gave him because he didn't even try to continue.

"I have an important job for you to do at home," Bramble said, then let his voice rise to the fairy range. "I need you to tell your mother that I need recharging. I will come and ask her myself, but if she is prepared, I will not need to spend time convincing her."

Thistle bobbed up to kiss his forehead. "I will make sure she is ready."

Proud of his solution to the treasure problem, Bramble flitted to the door and waved goodbye to his children.

"What are we waiting for?" he called back to Lionel and

Fernlight. "The sooner we get there, the sooner we'll be eating and drinking."

"Can you ask Mark if he does take-out?" Kim called. "If he can, bring back some food for us."

That would be something for Fernlight and Lionel to deal with. A fairy cannot carry such big things as meals for large people.

CHAPTER FORTY-FIVE

Lionel noticed a few humans in the crowd at Banks'. He hoped Mark took care with who he let in the door. Maybe he should tell Mark about the killer and about the disruption spells. But perhaps it was better to keep things confidential until they solved the cases.

No sign of Raj, but it had not been quite a half hour, so they would wait.

"No alcohol," Fernlight said. "And probably no food until Raj joins us. We may need to leave quickly if his news is a clue."

"I can go look for him," Bramble said. "There's no point in being in Banks' if we can't drink or eat or socialize."

Lionel guided them to a table near the door. "I'll let Mark know we're waiting for Raj. I think we need to wait until he's officially late."

"Who will go to the court?" Bramble asked, settling on the back of the chair. "I don't have the patience to deal with sidhe."

"If he doesn't join us here, I'll go," he said. "You can visit your wife and Fernlight can go with Raj back to the office."

They would need to go outside and walk to the front entrance of the court. It was only a handful of blocks away. The tunnel leading from Banks' would be faster, but taking that route carried no guarantee that Maeve would open the door at the other end. And that dark passage was where Quinn lost his eyesight.

"Good," Bramble said.

Lionel remembered the last time he'd been with a fairy in Maeve's presence. It must take a lot of energy for a fairy to deal with the sidhe in their court. Maeve would either ignore Bramble or say things to make him feel inferior. He wondered why the other magical folk didn't have this status conflict. Perhaps because the fairy folk were the only ones who came in three different kinds? Sidhe, courtly and manipulative, fairy, bright, emotional and excitable, brownies, practical and curious. Something to think about when they had time. Lionel waited for Mark to finish with his customer and then told him about Raj.

When he returned to the table, Bramble was pacing the top. "It is now two minutes past the time. I should go find him."

The back door opened as Lionel was about to speak. Three sidhe came through, looked at their table, then turned away. Had Maeve done something to Raj? If so, he would find out when he went to the court.

"Give him a bit more time, Bramble," Fernlight said. "Even with directions, it is hard for a human to find Banks' the first time."

Lionel's senses twitched. "Yes, it is hard, but Raj should be here. He said a half hour, but HOP-D is only fifteen minutes away. Let's go out and try a tracker spell. If he's lost, then we can bring him in." He stood and started for the door, Bramble flying ahead of him. Fernlight didn't join them.

"Are you staying here?" he asked.

"No. I wanted to see if they expected Leith to join them." She nodded to the table where the three sidhe still watched.

"You think Maeve has spies on us?" Bramble asked. "I will go and ask them."

"No," Lionel said before Bramble could leave. "Let's see if they follow us. We can find out later if we need to worry."

"True," Bramble said, flying toward the door. "Sidhe are always sneaky. We should go find Raj."

In the alley, Lionel found a gap between two Dumpsters and cast the tracker spell.

The mist rose from the leaves and twigs, but simply spiraled straight up, not even testing a direction.

"Is your magic broken?" Bramble asked. "Did the sidhe do something bad?"

Lionel called the mist back into the ingredients. "It is working, but Raj is hidden."

Fernlight pulled out her phone. "Perhaps Kim can use human tracking methods."

It only took a few seconds for Kim to find a signal from Raj's phone, two blocks away. "It's gone, though. He turned it off and maybe pulled the SIM card. Or someone did."

"Human," Lionel said. "Magical folk would not know to do that."

"I can get the last numbers he called," Kim said. "I'll call you as soon as I have it. Maybe an hour at most."

"We'll check the court for Leith," Fernlight said. "Maybe it is about what they found at HOP-D."

"Let me know," Kim said and ended the call.

"There is another option," Lionel said. "Mamoru's friend. The secretive one."

"Who?" Fernlight asked.

"I forgot we didn't tell you. He is a kind of spy and he offered to help us. I need the phone number for him. I already have the password."

He left a message for Mamoru and ended the call.

"The sidhe didn't follow," Bramble said. "Should we confront Maeve?"

Fernlight shook her head. "Easier to confront the sidhe inside." She opened the door. Lionel followed her through, eyes focused on the table near the back door. The sidhe were gone.

CHAPTER FORTY-SIX

"Maybe Kim found the people Raj talked to on his phone," Bramble said.

Fernlight looked at her phone. "We need to go outside again. I have no signal to use to find out if she has called back. But it hasn't been long enough."

Bramble rushed to the ally, hoping Raj was coming toward the pub. No luck. Lionel and Fernlight joined him, with Fernlight staring at the screen still.

"He isn't here," Bramble said. "Something is very wrong."

"I still can't find a signal," she said. "Oh. Now I do."

Kim had left a message. Fernlight played it on speaker.

Mamoru had all the phones registered to the agency, so I just had to look online. After he called you, Raj ordered pizza. But that's weird since he was expecting to eat at Banks'. He talked to that guy, Grant Norman, and two unknown numbers.

"Call her to find out who owns the unknown numbers," Bramble said.

Lionel put his hand over the phone. "I'm sure if she was able to identify the people easily, she wouldn't call them unknown."

"We need Leith," Fernlight said. "He will know why Raj ordered food, and he needs to be with us when we go to Mr. Norman and interview him."

She made it sound like more than asking questions. Bramble imagined they would tie up the human and cast spells to make him tell them all the truth. The image made his wings happy.

"We need a plan," Fernlight said. "Bramble, stop whizzing around. We need more people and more information. I'll start with Leith. If he's still at the court, I'll leave a message because Maeve won't let the phones work in there. Then we'll call Rhodri. I want a bigger team to go to this Norman person. If he kidnapped Raj, we'll rescue him — but it's too soon to be very worried about Raj. There will be an explanation for his absence. Then we will call Agnes to see what magic we can use to interview the man."

Bramble hated this plan. "Agnes shouldn't be holding us back. She said her work wouldn't get in the way."

Fernlight didn't answer. She was talking to Leith. "Join us outside Banks'. We are going to interview someone. Why did Raj order pizza?"

She thanked Leith a moment later and ended the call. "For the people at HOP-D. Leith said it was a good idea because we need friends in the human teams."

Fernlight pressed the button for Rhodri. "Meet us at Mr. Norman's home."

As she finished that call, Bramble saw Leith slip out of Banks' door.

"Maeve thanks you for the update, but as expected, she is unhappy with our progress." Leith looked right at Bramble. "You need energy," he said.

"Yes, I am going home in a minute to refresh my power." He hoped his children had done a good job of preparing Thorn so the treasure would be waiting.

"I know the fairies believe the source of their power is secret," Leith said, "but we are aware of the truth."

Bramble flew right into his face. "Do not say anything! You sidhe promised to forget so we would not punish you!" It was long before he was born, almost five years, but every fairy knew the story of the great sidhe robbery.

"It is not possible to forget," Leith said. "And Lionel was there at the time. We promised not to tell anyone."

"Then don't!"

Leith smiled a sneaky sidhe smile. "I bring the event up because I can offer aid. I have this chain infused with sidhe power that should be compatible." He held out a short, thin sliver chain.

"You want to control me!"

"The magic will work even if the clasp is open." He touched one of the links and the chain became a long silver snake.

"Bramble, try it," Lionel said. "I'm sure it's not a trick, but I will free you if I am wrong."

Leith held out the pretty length of silver. Bramble could feel the power. Not as pure as fairy, but better than convincing Thorn. "I will put this in my pocket." He snatched the chain before Leith could take it away.

"It will work for a couple of hours," Leith said. "When it is drained, please keep the jewelry. Perhaps a gift to your wife?"

Thorn would like the pretty necklace, Bramble thought as the metal slithered into his pocket and curled up. He filled with energy right away. If this was a sidhe trick, he couldn't see the trap. If it wasn't? Well, this one sidhe might be safe to like and trust.

"Thank you," he said. "Let's go."

Fernlight didn't move. She was talking on the phone. Kim might have called with more names.

"Just a second, Agnes," Fernlight said, then tapped the speaker on the phone. "Go ahead, we can all hear you."

"As can anyone walking by," Agnes said.

Lionel crushed a peanut shell. "We have privacy."

"You wanted to know what kind of magic you can use on this subject."

Agnes doesn't sound like she is going to say go ahead and use all the spells you want to.

"You can't use any. The brownies can probably search, since they understand the rules of permission."

They don't ask permission.

"Be careful, because there isn't enough to get a search warrant. But also, because if this is the killer, he's dangerous."

"We have dealt with many dangerous people," Bramble said. "And he might have kidnapped Raj. And maybe the minister too."

"Two," Fernlight said. "Two dangerous people. And we always take care. Thank you, Agnes."

Fernlight ended the call and Lionel ended the privacy.

"Why did you thank her?" Bramble asked. "She didn't give us any help."

"It's polite, and she cares that we don't get hurt," Fernlight said.

"Can we go now? To interview this man who will be our killer. I promise we will be very careful when we arrest him."

As he followed Fernlight out of the alley, he heard her say, quietly, "We don't arrest people."

CHAPTER FORTY-SEVEN

The Grant Norman human doesn't look like a bad man, Bramble thought. He let them into his home and offered them tea. Everyone said no, even though a spoon of honey would be welcome. Good thing the chain in his pocket was giving him strength.

Bramble floated to the ceiling so he could see everything that went on. If the brownies were not already busy, it would be good to tell them to search here. Even Agnes had said it was okay. But they were looking for the spell in the minister's house.

Leith and Rhodri sat across from Grant Norman. Fernlight wanted them to do the interview because she said people felt comfortable with their confidence and no one noticed their subtlety. Bramble was confident that he would simply ask the questions so they could finish fast.

"Mr. Norman," Rhodri said, "thank you for giving us your time."

"Did you find Minister Chan?" Grant Norman asked. He sounded concerned, but he didn't look like he was.

Bramble's ears were very sensitive. Mr. Norman was only saying the words he thought should be said.

"Not yet," Rhodri said. "This meeting is about something different. You made a call to our colleague Raj Mander this afternoon."

"I don't believe so," Mr. Norman said.

Leith smiled like the sneaky sidhe always did before doing something nasty. "We have the records. Is this your phone number?" He passed a slip of paper to Mr. Norman.

"It is, but I didn't speak to anyone named Raj." He passed the paper back to Leith.

Bramble wondered why the sidhe used magic to put the note back in his pocket.

"The call lasted only a few moments," Rhodri said. "Perhaps you didn't know who you called?"

Mr. Norman sat back in his chair and held his hands in his lap like he couldn't be sure they would stay there otherwise. Subtle wasn't going to work, but Bramble didn't want to break his promise to Fernlight.

There were many things in the room. This human liked to collect things. He had some pretty glassware. A few weird masks made out of wood, straw and beads hung on the walls. Bramble kept his ears listening to the conversation as he slowly floated around, looking for just the right thing.

"It is possible I called the wrong number," Mr. Norman said. "In fact, now that I think of it, I was calling a messenger service and did connect with someone. That must have been your friend. I simply hung up."

The bookshelves lined two walls, meeting at the corner where ornaments filled the space that books wouldn't fit. On the middle shelf, a pile of smooth stones looked like just the thing Bramble wanted.

"Did you connect with the courier?" Leith asked like he was worried Mr. Norman didn't get his package delivered.

"I don't see how that is your business," Mr. Norman said.

The words came out harsh enough that Bramble's wings started to vibrate him higher up the wall. He reached out and carefully took a black stone with a gray stripe from the pile and slipped it next to the chain.

"I would like you to leave now," Mr. Norman said in response to something Bramble missed.

"Indeed," Rhodri said. He sounded disappointed in Mr. Norman.

"If you want to talk to me again, make an appointment. I'll bring my lawyer with me."

When they stood on the sidewalk again, Bramble asked, "Why didn't you touch the paper when Grant Norman gave it back?"

"Do you think he noticed?" Leith asked. "I understand the reason we are not supposed to do magic without Agnes's involvement, but I thought a little tracking powder might be useful. I activated it when I passed the note. When he returned it, I couldn't contaminate the spell with my touch."

"Agnes will not like that," Lionel said.

"She doesn't need to know," Leith said. "We can find a way to explain anything we find, I'm sure."

Sometimes sneaky comes in handy.

"And what did you take from the shelf?" Leith asked. "I suppose thieving is considered fair play?"

And sometimes it does not.

Bramble showed the stone in his hand. "Perhaps a spell can give us an idea of what Mr. Norman was doing at the time he called Raj."

Fernlight groaned. "We seem to be unable to follow a few rules," she said. "If Mamoru thought we were getting better, he's going to be disappointed. But perhaps when we succeed all will be forgiven."

CHAPTER FORTY-EIGHT

"A truth spell," Lionel said, surprising himself with the idea. One second he was worrying about Agnes and Mamoru being angry, and then the spell idea shoved everything else out of his mind.

"The stone should only have facts," Leith said. "Truth is very different to fact."

"If the stone only shows us facts, we might be inundated. What if it's been there for years?" Lionel glanced around the area again. A few people were out on the street. More worrying was the number of windows looking out at them. And Grant Norman was only a few feet away. "We should go somewhere else."

Fernlight suggested the park a few blocks away. "The trees will give us cover."

The park covered a large area and Fernlight was right, there were plenty of places where the trees were dense enough to hide them even from the tenants of the tall apartment buildings around the edges.

Settling under an old Fir tree whose branches touched the

ground and made a shelter inside, Leith created a circle to protect them from prying eyes and ears.

"Cast the spell," Bramble said. "Then we can go back and make Mr. Grant Norman tell us why he is lying about talking to Raj."

"Don't forget he's connected to both of our cases," Rhodri said. "Maybe a coincidence, but I find it difficult to stretch my credulity to believe that."

"What will happen to the stone when you cast the spell?" Leith asked.

"Nothing," Lionel said.

"I mean the records it holds," Leith said. "The stone has been sitting on the shelf absorbing the activity going on around it. Will that be removed when we ask for the truth, or will everything still remain?"

The world did not get any simpler by itself, Lionel thought. No wizard would destroy information. The sidhe didn't know enough about wizard magic. The realization came with frustration and relief. The sidhe would likely use any information they found to their benefit.

"Everything will remain. We will probably need to replay the spell for Mamoru and Agnes at least to prove we are not manipulating the information."

"What exactly are you going to ask?" Rhodri pointed to the stone now sitting in the center of the circle. "While we may have the opportunity to try many times, we are not blessed with the luxury of time."

Lionel sorted through the ideas that flooded his mind. Half of his attention was being dragged to the future uses of such a spell. If it could be made into a tool for humans to use... No, that could wait. Perhaps releasing the locks on Heath's spell book had somehow let out his influence, his ideas of helping humans with magic-infused items. "We have three current cases," he finally said. "The most urgent is finding Raj, correct?"

The others agreed.

"Then I think we should ask for the truth about Mr. Norman's contact with Raj. When we find him, we can ask about the other crimes."

"And if Mr. Norman was telling the truth," Fernlight said. "That way we don't waste our time with him. Is your tracking spell working, Leith?"

"Yes, it is active, but he is not. Whatever he is doing, it is at his home."

Lionel pulled out a small package of the activating chalk he kept in his pocket. A useful tool to conserve his energy and didn't require him to think what charms he needed in advance.

He took a pinch of the powder and sprinkled it on the stone. "We would learn the truth about the phone call between Raj Mander and Grant Norman." He added the phone numbers and time from the report Kim sent.

The chalk slid from his fingers to cover the stone. Lionel felt the tiny pull of power as the spell activated. The powder shifted and swirled on the surface of the object, then rose. A letter formed, then another, and suddenly the magic tether between Lionel and the spell broke. The chalk fell to the earth.

"This is bad," Bramble said. "Just like the other spells we tried, failure."

"Let me keep trying," Lionel said.

After four attempts, they still had no information.

"As Bramble said, this is bad." Lionel blew the chalk away from the stone and stared at it. "I guess we don't need to worry about Agnes being angry. If magic isn't working, there's no risk to the case."

Bramble held out his hand and blinked. A small blackberry bush appeared. He blinked again and his palm was empty. "Magic still works," he said. "Fairy magic, anyway."

Leith sent shining balls flying around their heads. "Sidhe magic too. I do not think the problem is magic. It is this case, these cases."

"I agree," Fernlight said. "If magic had ceased, we would know immediately. I would dissolve into the earth."

"You would learn my age," Leith said, smoothing his jacket. "I am not eager for that."

"So now what?" Lionel asked. "Do we admit defeat?"

Fernlight asked Leith to break the circle. "Raj still needs to be found, the cases solved, and whoever ordered Heath's murder needs to be caught. We need to talk this over."

"Just us?" Lionel asked. He was out of ideas, but perhaps the others were not.

"I'll call Kim," Fernlight said. "The brownies are still busy, and they can find us when they are done."

Leith stood and brushed debris from his trousers. "Perhaps Banks' would be a better place than this?"

CHAPTER FORTY-NINE

Agnes stood behind Kim in the dirty alley in Gastown. Not a place she would usually go, even with someone as capable as the woman in front of her. The door looked so rusty it couldn't keep anyone out, but Kim reached for where a handle should be, and one appeared. She pulled and stepped into a noisy, warm, cheerful bar.

"The disguise on the door is new," Kim said. "Mark must need higher security. I'm allowed, and I guess I can bring you. Otherwise, we wouldn't be able to get inside."

Behind the bar, a creature of stone and nightmares filled a beer stein for a sprite. "A troll?" Agnes asked. "He owns the bar?"

"Best beer and food I've ever had," Kim said. "Our table is over there." She pointed to where most of the agency's investigators sat staring at them.

"You didn't tell them I was coming?" Agnes didn't regret insisting on accompanying Kim because something told her if progress had been made on the case, a lot of magic had been used.

"They'll get over the shock," Kim said. "Go ahead. I'll let

Mark know who you are and put in our order. I recommend the stew and a beer."

"Stew would be perfect," Agnes said. "I think tea would be better. I think I should keep a clear head."

Kim laughed and went to talk to the bartender. Agnes took a deep breath and wove through the patrons to join Fernlight and team.

"Why are you here?" Bramble asked.

Agnes pulled out a chair and sat. The fairy's bluntness was refreshing most of the time; the lack of tact also wore her down after a while.

"I was at the office when you called Kim," Agnes said. "I thought this would be a great opportunity to touch base. You've made progress?"

Kim sat beside Agnes. "Mark says the food will be here in a few," she said. "I see Raj is still missing."

Bramble glared at Leith. "Yes, and Leith, you didn't tell us what you found at HOP-D. What are you hiding?"

"I wish I were hiding something," Leith said. "Unfortunately, I was summoned by my queen for an update before we finished. Queen Maeve is not willing to take a backseat, and I must obey her commands."

"How do we know she didn't kidnap him?" Bramble was not going to just let the sidhe do as they wanted.

"She did not," Leith said, his voice cold, and Bramble's wings started flicking. "She has no reason to take a human, no matter how charming."

Rhodri placed his beer mug on the table before saying, "Bramble, it makes no sense for Maeve to interfere in such a way. But she is disrupting our progress. There must be a way to build a working relationship that allows you to concentrate on the case, Leith. Maeve may be demanding, but she is not unreasonable."

"We don't have time for that," Bramble said. "If you can't help us find Raj, why are you here?"

"Bramble, that is enough," Fernlight said. "We are all worried. It is not Leith's fault."

The fairy floated to sit on the back of Fernlight's chair, then crossed his arms and folded his wings back. "He is not helping either."

"He restored your power," Fernlight said in a tone that closed off any further comments.

Lionel reached to help the waiter distribute bowls and plates. Agnes's tea smelled of herbs and even the scent refreshed her. The stew added a rich aroma of root vegetables and red meat.

Bramble accepted a spoonful of honey and seemed to lose his annoyance with the first slurp.

"What was Raj doing when you left?" Lionel asked. "Perhaps that will help."

"Looking into their records for any possible crimes that could be related to our dead body and investigating the victim's background. Much as we do with magic, but slower."

Finally, an opportunity to ask about spells. Perhaps it wouldn't result in Bramble becoming angry again. Agnes was getting weary of explaining why she wasn't the enemy.

"And while you were investigating this Grant Norman in person, what magic did you use?" she asked. She tasted the food, as delicious as the aroma promised. The notebook would stay in her bag for now. Perhaps if it felt more like a discussion than an interview, no one would take offense.

"None of our spells worked," Lionel said. "There is something very wrong with this case. Someone is blocking our efforts. That means either one of us magical folk directly, or one of us sold a human a protection charm stronger than most people would need."

"What kind of spells did you use?" she asked again. "Even

if they didn't work this time, I can include them in my recommendations, perhaps classify them by group, like various tracking spells, information gathering, things like that."

Bramble put his honey spoon down and walked across the table to stand in front of her. She picked up her tea and sipped to avoid prompting him and getting the wrong reaction.

"We cast a truth spell on one of the things he collects."

He glanced at the sidhe. To hide a spell, or to indicate Leith should let Bramble tell the story? Leith didn't add anything.

"It should have given us information on what Grant Norman said to Raj when he called him. Grant Norman lied about the phone call."

Agnes didn't ask how they obtained the whatever object they'd used; magic was her mandate, not mundane evidence gathering. "Is that all, or is there something more you expected?"

This time Lionel spoke. "I expected the spell to show us what happened, perhaps written it out. I did the spell right. And the magic tried to work but dissolved before it even got started."

"It's not the first spell to have failed lately," Leith said. "It is as Lionel said, someone provided a protection on whoever we need to find. Whether that is the murderer or someone who knows what happened, we don't know."

Despite her determination to stay out of the investigation, Agnes found herself interested in the details. "Is it possible magic is fading?"

"We still feel the power," Rhodri said. "It is not weakened. But it is not just the spells being blocked that concerns me. The same feeling, I think humans would call it evil, we found in the minister's office, was in his home, too. We are waiting for the brownies to report."

"I hope you find the answer soon," Agnes said. "The only upside to spells failing is it makes the whole thing more relatable to us humans. Our tools don't always help either."

"What do we do next?" Kim asked. "Instead of solving the cases, we seem to just complicate everything."

CHAPTER FIFTY

Bramble flew around the office, trying to burn off some of the excess energy coursing through his veins. The sidhe jewelry power was too much, but if he said anything about his reaction, Leith would probably think it a compliment.

"What now?" he asked. Everyone was back in the office. Well, everyone except Raj who needed to be found, and the brownies. It was very odd how long they were taking to search the minister's house. What if they'd been kidnapped too? How would someone keep an entire horde captive?

"One thing we haven't done yet is try to connect all the bits of information we've found," Kim said. "We just got most of it. Normally we would write everything on the board and then brainstorm links to see if anything makes sense."

Agnes pulled up a chair and sat with them like she was one of the team. "Do you know a spell that will work for that?" she asked. "Sorting through and connecting facts is the human way. Any magic you use would be fine because the leads will need to be followed up."

Lionel rubbed his face like he needed to sleep. Bramble

floated over to check if he needed to rest, but all he saw was frustration. Yes, everyone felt that.

"I know a few," Lionel said in answer to Agnes's question. "I'm sure the druids do too, but magic is so unreliable in these cases, I think we should do it the human way."

Kim stood then flipped the whiteboard over to the blank side. "Let's hope that doesn't continue," she said. "Let's list what we found first. And I think we should include everything for all the cases."

"Why?" Bramble asked. "Won't it be confusing?"

"We already found one link," she said. "Grant Norman is on the list of possible suspects for both cases and he talked to Raj."

"Wait," Bramble said. "I forgot what I was thinking about earlier, but the brownies, they are usually very fast at searching, but we haven't heard from them in a long time."

Fernlight picked up her phone. "I hope we're not putting their names on the board." She sent a text, and her phone beeped with the reply right away. "They are almost done."

The relief he felt surprised him. Not because they were important to him; he didn't want to train new people to do what the brownies did, that's all. "So, they are not kidnapped too," Bramble said. "Good, we do not need more complications."

Kim wrote cases in the four corners of the whiteboard. Murder. Minister. Heath. Raj.

"What do we know?" she asked, holding the marker pen ready to record.

"Grant is in both lists from Heath's case," Rhodri said.

"And he called Raj. And there is definitely some kind of magic block around him." Bramble added before the others could say all the clues.

"There was a disruption charm at the minister's office, and I'm certain one in his home," Lionel said.

Kim wrote everything in the center of the board.

"With luck, the brownies found it," Leith said. "There was another name on both lists. Vivianne Braithwaite? Yes?"

Bramble buzzed to the papers spread over Kim's desk. He found the list of people who might be part of the *Sla Styrkur* place. Yes, he remembered seeing her name. Leith just said it first. "She is here. The woman who had the magical things."

"And she is the one we were unable to meet with when we followed the minister's movements," Rhodri said.

"We set an appointment for tomorrow," Lionel said.

Kim asked again for things to write on the wall. No one said anything, so she started to draw lines from the cases to the clues.

"Okay, for our case of the missing Raj, we only have Grant Norman," she said. "But for Grant Norman, we also found connections to Heath's case. For Vivianne, we can only link to Heath's case."

Bramble floated over to stare closer at the words. "You can link him to the blocking magic," he said. "And to the Vivianne woman, and to the dancing body, because that's what we asked about when we did the spell."

Kim stepped back from the board and read it again. "Not enough to get a search warrant anywhere."

CHAPTER FIFTY-ONE

"What are you doing?" Pit asked as the horde flowed into the office.

Bramble let Fernlight explain while he picked up another marker. That Vivianne person might also have the magic blocker in the objects she hid in her desk.

"Then we have things to add to the list of clues," Pit said. He reached into his brownie sack and pulled out a notepad. "We did not remove anything from the minister's home, but four things seem important."

Kim went back to the board and prepared to write.

"The disruption spell was on a piece of jewelry in Mae's bedroom. We informed her and wrapped it in a special brownie cloth that will contain the magic until the correct authorities can remove the charm safely. We suggest the druid for that task."

"Who is Mae?" Bramble asked. "And why were you so long?"

Pit lowered the notepad and stared at Bramble. "Mae is the minister's wife. She was very happy we found the charm, and she provided us with refreshments when we finished our search. As you know, that created an obligation for us to clean the house. It took time to convince her to accept we would do our job. Her house is now cleaner than she has ever seen it before. We also suggested a team of brownies would be helpful in clearing out all the things she collected. The house is quite full. She declined."

Bramble nodded for Pit to continue reporting. The brownie glared at him but looked at the notebook again. "Found marijuana cigarettes in her closet. I suppose that is less helpful. A collection of letters containing the two names on your board." He reached into the bag and pulled out a gold watch. "Mae allowed us to take this to possibly track her husband."

Bramble watched as Kim wrote the last of the clues and drew the lines. "What did the letters say?"

"From Grant Norman, a letter saying he was happy to recommend Ivan Sawchuk as a volunteer. Our dancing body worked as an intern for Mr. Norman. And there was a second letter from him introducing the Vivianne Braithwaite woman as a potential ally. It did not say what the minister required an ally for, and since he works with Maeve, we were unable to guess."

Kim made the last connections and stood back. Bramble wished he'd been the one to find all the clues, but at least now they knew what to do next: arrest Mr. Norman.

"Enough for a search warrant on Norman," Kim said. She was looking at Agnes.

"Only on him," Agnes said. "I suggest Lionel and Rhodri take some reinforcements to their appointment with the woman."

"Raj will be there; I know it," Bramble said. "Let's go."

Agnes picked up the phone. "I will call Mamoru about the warrant. Please don't enter the premises until I bring it or call you."

"Ask for the office and house," Kim said.

Bramble didn't want to wait until they decided to stop talking. "Kim, do you still have the fairy path charms?"

She nodded but didn't look particularly happy. Bramble didn't care. They could get within a block of Grant Norman's house in minutes using the paths.

CHAPTER FIFTY-TWO

Bramble wanted to be in front of Grant Norman's door when the warrant came. In fact, he wanted to be inside and take the brownies with him, but Kim said no. They all must wait on the street a block away so he wouldn't suspect anything and maybe destroy evidence. So now they sat on the ground and waited.

"What about the spy?" Lionel asked suddenly. "Mamoru's secretive telephone contact."

Fernlight pulled out her phone and looked at a list of numbers. "He hasn't called back. I made contact as Mamoru instructed a while ago."

Bramble swooped over. "Try again. Maybe he didn't see that you called."

Kim pulled her jacket close around her. "What are we going to ask if he does call back?"

"Are you cold?" Bramble asked. "Lionel, don't you have a warming charm for her?"

"That's kind of you, Bramble," Kim said. Lionel handed her a bay leaf and told her to put it in her pocket.

"I don't want you falling ill and delaying us," he said.

"Good thinking," Kim said. She smiled, "I would hate that too."

"Well?" Bramble asked Fernlight. "What do we need that we can't get ourselves now that we know about Grant Norman?"

Fernlight ended her call. "If he bothers to call us back, perhaps he can find some information we can use to make Mr. Norman talk to us."

"Or perhaps find Raj," Leith said.

"If brownies can't find him, no one can," Pit said. "How long must we wait? Brownies are not used to standing around."

"Until we hear from Agnes," Kim said. "She's asking for a warrant on his home and business. We should split up. We can keep in touch by phone, but we don't want him warning anyone if he gets a chance."

"There is not much in the business," Rhodri said. "I'll go. Perhaps I'll notice if anything has changed."

"If Lionel and I accompany Rhodri," Leith said, "that leaves our suspect facing a sprite, a fairy, and a human. It might send a good message."

"I will send Shade and half the horde with you," Pit said.

"How can you be sure he's still at home?" Kim asked. "He could be at the office or even out of the country."

Bramble's wings were taking him around in circles. Where was Agnes? Would she come to them? Would she call and say she had the warrant? This was dangerous talk if she was coming. "Leith put a tracker on him. Agnes doesn't know yet."

"It's more of a tag than a tracker," Leith said. "I am aware of his location when I think about him. I cannot follow his tracks. He is at home. At this time of night, most humans are sleeping."

"That could come in handy if approved," Kim said.

A car pulled up and Agnes got out. She had a paper in her hand. They could search now and soon the cases would all be solved!

"I made two copies," she said, handing the papers to Fernlight. "If anyone is at the office, it will go more smoothly if you can show the warrant."

Bramble took one of the copies and handed it to Leith. "We will search everything, and we will arrest him when we find the proof."

"You can search his house, the grounds, and any outbuildings," Agnes said. "You can only look for evidence he is involved in any of the cases."

"I don't understand," Pit said. "If we can search everything, then why is there a restriction?"

Kim reached for the other copy of the warrant. "Because it is not a fishing expedition. If we find evidence he's selling street drugs or smuggling computer parts, we can't use it."

"You can inform the police," Agnes said. "They will be very happy to take on the mundane crimes."

Pit finished talking to his horde and they broke into two littler hordes. Shade stepped forward. "And the office? What can we search there?"

"His premises, any common areas on the same floor, and the lobby," Agnes said.

"And if we find drugs or evidence of smuggling in these common areas?"

"Tell the police. It might have nothing to do with your suspect."

"Let's get going," Bramble said.

"I'll leave you to it," Agnes said. "I have the feeling that my presence might affect the activities."

She drove away and the two groups prepared to split up. Bramble struggled to wait until they finished. But it only took a moment.

Lionel led the office team to the nearest magical path.

Fernlight's phone rang.

"Wait," she said. "Maybe this is the spy."

She answered.

"I understand." She ended the call.

Bramble waited a whole second before he asked, "Was it him? What did he say?"

Fernlight moved to walk to the house. "He's been investigating already. He said there's a link between Mr. Norman and another name. But he wasn't going to tell us because it would mean he was too entangled, whatever that means."

"It means he doesn't want to be dragged into court," Kim said. "It's a good tip."

CHAPTER FIFTY-THREE

Bramble hovered behind the others as Fernlight knocked on Grant Norman's front door. If the human was going to hurt someone, it would be better for him to get one of the larger people. Even Kim would be able to defend herself. Fairies were better off coming to the rescue than being rescued. He looked for Pit, but the brownie was already gone.

"Knock again," Kim said. "We can't break down the door with this kind of warrant, and we don't want to scare him into calling whoever he's connected to anyway."

"It is quite late," Fernlight said.

Bramble zipped to the window. Maybe he would be able to see through a crack in the curtains. Before he found a gap, he heard footsteps coming down the stairs. He flew back to his safe position and waited.

The door opened far enough for a human face to peek at them. Kim held out the paper, but the man didn't take it.

"We have a warrant to search the premises." Kim pushed the door, but it didn't move. "Mr. Norman, we are coming in to execute the warrant. Please don't make us force the issue."

"You woke me up," he said. "Give me a minute."

He tried to close the door, but Kim pushed again with no success.

Bramble touched the sidhe chain in his pocket to pull a little extra power. "Kim, move away from the door, please." He didn't want to hurt her, and he needed all his concentration to keep the spell gentle enough not to break anything but strong enough to make the door move.

He threw the spell. It left a trail of fairy powder as it passed. When the spell hit the door, it pushed hard enough to move Grant Norman too.

"Nicely done, Bramble," Kim said. She led them into the lobby where a wide set of stairs went up to the second floor and another smaller one down.

"You are welcome to observe," Kim said. "Or you can wait here. I don't know how long we will be."

"What are you looking for?" As he asked the question, Grant Norman opened the folded warrant that Kim had forced into his hand. "Wait, you are searching my office too?"

"Yes," Fernlight said. "Another team is there."

"This is because I called a wrong number?" He tossed the warrant on a chair. "Why do you think I know anything about dead bodies and missing people?"

"I suggest you call your lawyer," Kim said. "We don't need to answer your questions, but you will answer ours."

"It's almost midnight," Grant said. "My lawyer won't be awake."

Kim looked around. "Are the brownies at work?" she asked Fernlight.

"Yes, we are on all the floors," Pit said, suddenly popping into the room. "The outside will come next."

"Maybe I should call him," Grant Norman said. "You have no right to infest my house with vermin."

Pit drew himself up and stared at the man. "We are not vermin. Many people value our services. Criminals do not, I suppose." He marched away and disappeared around the corner of the lobby.

"Maybe I should call someone else," Grant Norman said. "My lawyer isn't the most influential person I'm acquainted with."

Kim looked at him and then turned to Fernlight. "Do we have a spell that prevents him from doing anything like that?"

"I don't, and I don't think anyone other than a wizard might have one."

Bramble shook his head when Kim looked at him. "We can let him call the lawyer and then put him in a stasis spell."

Bramble expected her to say it was a great idea, but she just thought for a few seconds. "No, I'll guard him. I'm not going to find what we need since it's likely to be magic."

She ushered Grant Norman into the living room and made him sit on one of the comfy chairs. "You search. When you need to look in here, I'll move him."

"We found something," a brownie announced. "Please come to the basement."

Kim nodded at them and turned to watch Grant Norman. Bramble joined Fernlight and the brownies in the basement, trying not to remember the last time he was in a basement and trapped with the spell that didn't want to die. "I can ask the fairies in the garden about anything hidden," he said.

"We already did that," Pit said. "Nothing. The man doesn't go there."

Another strike against him. "What did you find?"

Pit picked up a pencil and pushed a blue ribbon across the floor toward Fernlight. "You will need to put this somewhere safe," he said. "You might be big enough to handle the effect, but a brownie just gets caught like in a net."

The ribbon was fraying on the end. It didn't look threatening, but it was definitely a bad charm. Like Lionel and Rhodri said about the beads. Bramble could feel the spell urging him to get mad at the brownies. He reached into this pocket for the bags his wife had made of bramble threads. "Push it in here," he said, holding the mouth of the bag open. "This will stop the magic getting to us."

When the ribbon was safely in Fernlight's possession, Bramble looked around the room. He noticed that there were a lot of drawings on the walls. Not of people, but patterns. Some of them were harmless, but others looked like the patterns wizards painted in the chalk circles they used to call the spirits. "Did you find anything else?"

"Yes, this," Pit said like he was presenting a prize. "I think this is what the spy meant."

On the floor sat a file folder. Inside was a list of names. The same names that were on the list about *Sla Styrkur*.

CHAPTER FIFTY-FOUR

Lionel missed Shade slipping into the office with the horde. Perhaps she was still in the lobby. There'd been no one to show their warrant to, and that was fine because it also meant no one to argue with them.

The office looked the same as earlier. He pushed the door shut behind him as he entered. The spell he used to unlock the door kept it closed while they searched, but if they needed to leave fast, the door would still open.

"There aren't many places to leave something that could solve our cases," Leith said. "Shall I try the other doors to see if there is a common space?"

Lionel didn't want to split the team, but it was a stupid fear. They would never get anywhere if he insisted they stay together. "Be quick," he said. "I'll take the desk he was using this afternoon. Rhodri, can you look in the others?"

Leith slipped out of the door.

"You think other people actually work here?" Rhodri asked. He opened the drawers in the closest desk. "Maybe I'm wrong." He pulled out a stack of envelopes and held them up.

Lionel sat at Grant Norman's desk. The drawers were locked when he tugged on them. He left them locked and looked around. *What does the man look at every day?* A computer on his desk, the other desks, the front of the office. Nothing to give him a hint.

He spun the seat, so he looked at the wall. A small shelf held a few awards and trinkets. No filing cabinet, no bookshelves. "I hope his house contains more promise," Lionel said as he cast the spell to open the drawers.

"Nothing in the lobby," Shade announced as she led the half-horde into the office. "Hmm. Not much to look at here either."

"Nothing in the bathroom," Leith said as he joined them. "Are we finished?"

Lionel poked through the contents of the desk. There was nothing to find. No emanations of destructive magic. No odd amulets. Nothing. "Do you think we can take the computer with us?"

Rhodri reached for the warrant sitting on the corner of Grant's desk. "Our warrant says we are looking for evidence. I presume we are supposed to take whatever we find away. Could we count the computer as evidence?"

It was probably splitting hairs, but Lionel didn't want to leave without a single item to show for the effort. "Can you try to break in and see if he kept anything interesting inside?" he asked Rhodri.

The druid took the laptop and placed it on the desk he'd finished searching. He turned the machine on, and a fan sounded. "Maybe."

"This is disappointing," Leith said. "Although I suppose we shouldn't have expected to find Raj and the minister tied up in the corner."

Lionel closed his eyes and sent his senses out into the area. Something in the far corner tickled his mind. He strode to where he felt the sensation the strongest. Whatever generated the feeling was under the floor.

"Shade, can one of the brownies get under the carpet?"

Shade led the half-horde to the corner. One of the brownies ran his hands across the floor and then whispered something to Shade.

"Yes," she said. "Lift the tile. Underneath is a floor panel we can lift too. The wires all fit in the floor so there is space. Not for a big person, but a brownie will have lots of room."

Leith and Lionel lifted carpet tiles until they exposed the entire floor panel. They raised that and placed it to the side. "Definitely something," Lionel said. "Be careful."

The brownie jumped down to land on the concrete below. Then he looked up and said something to Shade.

"You can talk to the big people, they are friends," she said back.

The brownie shook his head and ducked under a bundle of wires and disappeared.

"He said there is a bad thing nearby. He will find it so you can bring the pieces out. Do you have one of those containers to keep us safe?"

Lionel pulled out a velvet bag. "I guess we all need to start carrying these."

The brownie slipped back into view. He took a deep breath and looked at Shade. "It is a bundle of bones. I think maybe a mouse. It carries a charm for bad things." He pointed to a spot just beside Leith's foot.

The sidhe stepped back and then knelt. "Under this?" he asked, pointing to a strap that was holding the bundle of wires to one of the metal braces.

Shade and the half-horde nodded at the same time.

Lionel bent and used a finger to lift the strap with the wires. He was reluctant to touch the sad pile of bones he found, and not just because of the spell that was trying to grab at his temper.

Rhodri knelt beside him. "Should we leave it in place?"

Lionel shook his head. "We can't. We have to find out who created this. It is the same spell as we found in the minister's office. I'm becoming more convinced that we are only seeing a small part of whatever these magical crimes are about."

He rose and went to the closest desk. Inside he found a pair of scissors. They would work for tongs if he was very careful.

When the bones were safely inside the damping bag, Lionel pulled the drawstrings and tied them into a double knot. "We need to let Fernlight know." He pulled out his phone. "No signal. These are really not as helpful as I hoped."

Shade tugged his pant leg. "It will only take a few minutes for me to report. Wait here."

When she got to the door, it opened, and she squeaked as she jumped back. Lionel reached for a defensive charm but relaxed when he saw Pit standing in the doorway.

"You must come to the agency," he said. "We have found something."

Lionel hoped it was something more than a disruption spell. Otherwise, that would be four of them: the minister's office and home, and Grant Norman's office and home.

CHAPTER FIFTY-FIVE

"Are all our cases going to end up being linked?" Lionel asked as he looked at the whiteboard. Now the lines running from facts to cases intersected in every direction.

Kim looked away from the board and shook her head. "It is unusual, but I think what happened is all of these and your previous cases are really one big case. The crimes are just what we see of some kind of big network. Organized crime."

All the investigators sat around the office. The results on the board came from the bits of evidence they found.

"Where is Grant Norman?" Leith asked. "Interrogating him should be our priority. We need to learn who the link is. It cannot be everyone on the list; someone must be leading the group, planning the crimes."

"Mamoru picked him up and said they would question him at HOP-D," Fernlight said. "He is prepared to arrest him as soon as he has enough proof."

"I didn't agree," Bramble said. "We should question him. Magic is involved and magic will solve the case."

Fernlight turned to look at him. "That's not all, Bramble.

What happened when Mamoru said we cannot arrest him, and we would need human observers?"

The fairy's wings drooped. "I said we could wait."

I am glad we are not surrounded by humans.

"It's best that there are mostly magical folk," Lionel said. "We have four disruption charms in here. It's easier for us to protect Kim than it would be to resist the compulsion to fight and protect multiple humans who don't trust what we do."

"The horde is also grateful." Pit pointed at the board. "We should look at this information while we have time. It will only be a few hours before most humans become active."

"What is the most common thread?" Lionel asked.

Kim picked up the marker and pointed. "We found a lot of connections, but nothing seems to be common. There must be a missing piece that will tie it all together."

"Can we refine any of the information?" Leith asked. "Perhaps the common names. Who are they and what do we know about them?"

Kim circled four names. "We didn't find out anything about A. Jones or Della Moore from the list. We are sure Grant is involved with our murder victim, the missing minister, and Raj. We haven't been able to talk to Vivianne Braithwaite, but we know she owns magical objects, and by the way she talked to that person, she may be under a similar charm as the ones we found."

Lionel went to his computer. He couldn't search for A. Jones, too common a name, but Della Moore might be in the Internet. "Did anyone do a regular search?"

"Just the magical ones," Kim said.

Lionel typed a few keys. "Della Moore was arrested in France yesterday with her accomplice, Audrey Jones. They are charged with corporate espionage."

Rhodri circled their names with a different color marker.

"It is possible they are involved, but since they are not here, we can put them lower on our connections list."

"What about this Selwyn Morgan?" Kim asked.

"He is one of the dead ones," Bramble said. "When we did the spell and two of the bubbles were empty. I checked. He died six months ago. Industrial accident. What does that mean?"

Kim marked his name in the same color as the other two. "Possibly an accident with whatever magic we end up finding in these cases, but only two names remain. Grant Norman and Vivianne Braithwaite."

"But nothing we can prove. Nothing linking her to Grant Norman, or the minister, or Raj." Lionel recognized the sound of defeat in Fernlight's voice. If they were only missing one piece, it would need to be a very big one to break any of their cases.

"Let's look at this from another angle," Rhodri said. "The oldest crime is Heath's murder. If we start with that, what do we learn?"

Pit climbed up Lionel's desk and pushed him away from the keyboard. Lionel stood and went to the board.

"We know Heath was making magic into tools. Is it possible the disruption charms are his?"

"Did you find anything like that in his book?" Bramble asked.

Lionel shook his head. "There are charms, but nothing like the disruption magic. If we assume the idea came from Heath, we must assume another magical being is involved in creating the spell or turning the spell into something Heath didn't intend."

"I remember something in the list of his spells," Pit said.

"A charm to disrupt?" Fernlight asked. "That doesn't seem like Heath."

"No." Pit kept his eyes on the computer screen.

"What about the company?" Rhodri asked. "He was selling to some human corporation. That's how you found *Sla Styrkur*, right?"

"Mainly through the last case," Bramble said.

Lionel sighed. They'd made no progress. He had pulled all the spell titles out of the book for Pit to categorize. If Heath didn't create the disruption charms, who did? And did it matter if they knew?

CHAPTER FIFTY-SIX

"I found it," Pit said.

Bramble spun around from the board where all the words and lines were a jumble and stared at Pit. How had the brownie found an answer? He was just looking in the computer. Kim had done that and Lionel, and... Maybe he should have looked too.

The others were waiting for the brownie to speak. Bramble stopped the questions running around in his head. Now was listening time. He would make sure Pit had not cheated later.

"First, you know everything except one piece. Do we agree?" Pit said. The horde pooled on the floor beneath him and looked up, eyes eager.

"Yes," Leith said. "It feels as though a single missing connection is all we need."

"You have not looked at Heath's spell book as deeply as me," Pit said.

Lionel gave a little jerk of surprise. "You can read the spells? We must talk later. You could save me a lot of time."

"I cannot read how to do them, or the ingredients. I can

only read the name and purpose. You stopped with the names."

Bramble watched Lionel nod. Why didn't he get angry about the brownies prying into his wizard magic?

"What did you find?" he asked. "We do not have all day to listen to what you did."

Fernlight coughed and when Bramble turned to her, she frowned at him. Was he supposed to be polite to brownies too?

"It is important to hear the way I figured it out," Pit said. "I don't think you will understand otherwise. The information is complicated."

Kim picked up a new marker and waited at the board. There was not much space left for human writing, but maybe she could write small like a fairy.

"You heard from this spy, who may be a brownie, that you would find a link between our suspect Grant Norman, and one of the other suspects." Pit paused until everyone agreed.

"The board shows that there are tangles of links between the company, the people and the victims."

"Yes, we did that work," Bramble said. Then, remembering Fernlight's look, he added, "Please continue, but faster."

"The link must be the charms," Pit said. "It's the only really unknown clue. Who made them, why, and how?"

Kim circled the charms, making even more mess on the board. "Heath made them?" she asked.

"In a way," Pit said. "Here is where things get complicated. Humans are ingenious. They always want things to go smoothly with the least effort. They cannot do magic, and we must all cling to that belief because the alternative is frightening."

"Can't argue with you there," Kim said. "So, who made the charms?"

"Heath and Vivianne Braithwaite."

Bramble buzzed over to stand next to Pit. "Is she not a human?"

"She is a human. I said it was complicated."

Bramble looked around the room. He wasn't the only one ready to yell at Pit to tell them. Lionel, who would be most worried because he was a wizard like Heath, and had inherited all Heath's belongings, rubbed his forehead. Bramble saw frustration rise out of his body like a green mist. If Pit didn't explain fast, everyone was going to get just as upset. And upset people didn't think right. "Pit, we are not understanding. You must explain better. Then we can catch the killer and find Raj and the minister." He tried to keep his voice happy, but it did sound a bit annoyed in his ears.

"Heath made notes in his spell book about who commissioned the magical tools. He did a lot of work with many companies, so I think it is because he didn't want to forget. In the book are three spells for the same company. One is to create a kind of static but for emotions. He noted the use as to hide specific activities from observation by drones or other surveillance."

"Cameras," Kim said. "A good spell for people who don't want their picture all over the place."

"The second spell transferred the magic onto objects. What he intended was to sell a powder or paint that would carry the spell so he wouldn't use all his time making static charms."

Bramble's wings trembled at the thought of another spell that transferred magic. "Can someone use this powder to make someone magic?"

"No," Pit said. "Heath made it delicate. The magic would not survive being injected or eaten."

"And the third?" Kim asked. "I assume that's what you found, right? The link?"

"The third is a potion," Pit said. "The user would spray it in the air and for a short time, they would be undetectable."

Bramble took the marker from Kim's fingers. She was lost in thought or too scared to write. He put the three spells on the board. "Whoever put the charms in the minister's office and home could have walked in, put them in place, and left without anyone knowing."

"Yes," Pit said. "The spell would give them two or three minutes."

"This might also explain why we are unable to find Raj or the minister. A quick spray would cut us off from the trail."

"So, if we can find who has all three of these," Kim said, "we will know they're our perpetrator. Probably for every case on the board."

"Vivianne Braithwaite," Pit said. "The three companies that Heath listed are all in her name."

One person did all this? Bramble no longer cared who found the clue.

CHAPTER FIFTY-SEVEN

Lionel tossed the salt string in a wide circle. For the first time he felt doubt about Heath's efficiency plans. Yes, the circle was much faster when cast this way, but what unexpected use would a human find, or create?

"How do we know the spell will work?" Bramble asked as he landed on the ground. "So much of the magic isn't right because of that woman."

Lionel sat beside Leith as soon as the circle sealed. "That is why we are all in here. Between us, we should be able to craft a spell that will penetrate the block."

Rhodri was pulling items from his pockets and placing them on the ground. Leith sorted through a variety of jewelry and potion bottles.

"I find myself excited to do this new combined magic," Leith said.

"Is your tracker on Grant Norman working?" Rhodri asked.

"It appears to be, but we should probably check to make sure our allies at HOP-D continue to hold him."

Lionel added his charms to the pile in the center and

placed a lighter beside the ingredients. "I wonder if there is a form of tracking spell we can create to allow us to track each other."

"So we could find Raj?" Bramble asked. "This is a good idea. You are more like Heath than I thought. Just be more careful. Heath didn't understand how tricky humans are."

The final ingredients sat on the ground. Lionel considered the process. "I don't like to rush, but we have no choice. My thought is we start with a druid spell to locate her. If that works, we'll follow with wizard, sidhe, and fairy to strengthen the magic."

"And if it doesn't?" Leith asked.

"Then we try again," Bramble said.

"Yes, but we should have a logic to our attempts. I suggest our second spell be fairy magic aligned with my own. Our magic is subtle and may be a better combination."

Bramble cocked his head and Lionel hoped he was convinced that Leith meant no harm, and if so, maybe the trust would last for longer than a few minutes.

"Your spell on Grant Norman," Bramble said, "it worked even though one of those disruption spells tried to mess everything up."

"But we were there in person," Leith said. "We can't wait until we meet with this woman."

"No. You are both correct," Rhodri said. "However, we must start somewhere. Lionel, how can we help?"

After four attempts, the spell finally showed a location. Vivianne Braithwaite was at home; if she moved, any of them would feel a shift in their magic. Lionel only hoped they could trust the result.

He opened the circle to see Agnes standing at the door.

"It was the same kinds of spells that we used before," he said. "Nothing new, and we couldn't wait."

"So I understand," Agnes said. "It is possible we have to rethink our approach to this assessment."

She turned and joined the rest of the team, Bramble buzzing past her to land beside Fernlight in the main part of the office. Lionel stood aside to let Leith and Rhodri pass. What does she mean? Rethink the approach?

CHAPTER FIFTY-EIGHT

Agnes waited on the street outside Vivianne Braithwaite's home, the warrant on her phone. She touched the charm hanging beside her pendant. Traveling the magical paths was something she could do without. Kim's warning didn't prepare her for the feeling of being buried. The only positive was she could recommend the use of these paths as benign magic. Although, the creepy feeling she couldn't dismiss made it unlikely to catch on as a shared human and magical tool.

"Before we go in," Kim said, "Bramble and the brownies should check with the fairies and sprites in the garden."

"There are none," Bramble said. "I don't know how the garden survives, but I couldn't find magical power there."

"If we are right about her," Lionel said, "they probably left before she did something awful."

"No traps or hidden objects," Shade said. "Pit is leading the horde inside now."

Agnes stepped back to allow the investigators to do their job. As much as she wanted to stop this woman, her job was to observe. If things went wrong, she would act, but only then.

"Leith first," Kim said. "We don't know for sure she's the culprit, but charm is a good starting point."

Leith stepped to the door. "Thank you for recognizing my asset. I assure you I am also capable of force if charm does not work."

Agnes held her breath as Leith rang the doorbell. This was her first warrant delivery, but she'd heard some horror stories that started with 'then they opened the door.'

"She is coming," Shade said. "Shall I join Pit?"

"When we are inside," Fernlight said. "Stay with us until then."

The door opened and a woman poked out her head. Despite the fact that it was four a.m., she was fully dressed and made-up—her dark hair pulled back into a ponytail, her blue eyes bright, her sweater and trousers free of creases.

"Oh, my," she said in a soft voice. "So many magical folk on my doorstep. What can I do for you?"

Her pleasant words didn't ease Agnes's anxiety. Terrible threats can come from gentle voices.

"We are here with a warrant to search your home," Leith said. "We hope that you can assist in finding some missing people."

The woman smiled widely and opened the door. "I have no one hiding in here. Please, you are welcome to look."

Everyone followed Leith into the house. As the door shut behind her, Agnes realized the mistake. Someone should stay outside. If this was a trap, they had no way of calling for help. She scanned the floor for any of the brownies, but they were too good to be seen. Perhaps they were too wily to be trapped.

"Can I offer tea? Something to eat?" Vivianne asked. "I

feel so lucky you are here. I don't get to meet many of your kind."

Agnes winced at the words. None of the others seemed to care that the woman had designated them as other and lesser. She looked to Kim and saw her own reaction reflected in the way her body held tight. Perhaps it was a human thing to diminish the different.

"We should begin," Leith said. "I assure you we will be respectful." He introduced the team, not acknowledging the brownies' presence.

"Please do be careful," Vivianne said. "I keep some very personal items. Things that carry enormous sentimental value."

As the team dispersed, Vivianne turned to Kim and Agnes, her subtle movement blocking them from joining the search.

"May I ask why you are here? You are not magical and yet you are part of this team."

As if we shouldn't mingle with magical folk.

"I am consulting with them on legal issues," Agnes said. "If you don't mind, I need to join them."

Vivianne shifted again. Now Agnes would need to push her away so she could enter.

Kim stepped forward and Agnes saw her police training take over. The movement carried authority even out of uniform. "Ma'am, you can watch as we work, or you can wait in the living room until we've finished. Satisfying your curiosity is not part of the deal."

Vivianne stiffened. She looked over Kim's shoulder to Agnes and seemed to be assessing her odds in a fight. Then she relaxed. "Of course, you must find your missing people. I will wait in the kitchen."

Agnes watched her leave, still not relaxing. "We should keep an eye on her," she whispered. "Something is wrong."

"She is under observation," Kim said. "The horde is in the kitchen."

The floor was an open plan, giving Agnes a view of the kitchen from counter up. "I don't see anything."

"The good thing about brownies is they are impossible to see unless they choose it," Kim said. "And the other good thing is they are smarter than people give them credit for. Pit and I arranged for him to split off part of the horde to keep an eye on her no matter what."

"She wanted to get rid of us," Agnes said. The tension eased at the realization Kim had suspected a bad outcome from the start. "She wants the magical folk for something."

Kim grinned and moved to start searching the hall closet. "She's lucky we don't go. Everyone here is capable of defending themselves, and no one believes she fell for Leith's charming manner. Not even Leith."

CHAPTER FIFTY-NINE

The search was proving to be a waste. Lionel had no doubt that this woman committed every crime since Heath's death, and probably a few they didn't know about.

The team had been through her house thoroughly, starting with magical items they knew were in her hidden compartment in the room where she had her office. It was empty, as though she'd known they were watching earlier.

"Come to the kitchen," Shade said, popping up out of nowhere as usual. "We have something."

Lionel made his way up to the first floor and joined everyone crowding into the small space. Kim stood at the back of the room, blocking Vivianne from moving closer to the brownies on the counter.

"Make some space," Pit said. "Come in here so we can control her."

In a moment, Kim was left alone with Vivianne as the others crowded to the other side of the room. Pit's brownies placed four items on the counter.

"This is our proof," he said. "In a secret cupboard behind this one." He patted a thin door that ran beside the refrigerator. "These are the pieces of the disruption charm. I will not put them together. We do not need any bad emanations."

Lionel eased himself to the counter. A vial of powder, a tiny bottle of potion and a ribbon sat next to a container of seeds. He didn't need to touch them to know how it worked. "The ribbon is just a cloth," he said. "The seeds are the static spell, the powder, a spell to use as a medium to adhere the ground-up seeds to an object. The potion is a distraction spell of some sort."

Pit stood back. "We have solved the case."

"Hey!" Kim shouted as Lionel was about to ask someone to contact Mamoru.

Kim tried to swat something from Vivianne's hands. Another charm.

Lionel reached for the seeds and yelled for Kim to move back. The seeds hit Vivianne and she seemed to lose focus on what she was doing for a moment; long enough for Lionel to retrieve and cast a binding spell.

Vivianne regained her focus just as she lost the ability to move.

"Call Mamoru," Lionel said. "I will deal with her."

He trusted that the rest of the team would do what was necessary while he managed their prisoner. Stepping forward to check that the binding wasn't damaging the woman, he saw her hands move. The spell was disintegrating. Before he could stop her, Vivianne pulled another charm from her pocket. A portal.

Lionel reinforced his spell and called for Rhodri to help him.

CHAPTER SIXTY

Agnes pulled a chair to her corner and climbed on it to get a better angle for her phone. She'd started recording as soon as Pit called everyone to the kitchen. It would work for evidence, and recording the magic could help sell it as a tool for other investigations and court cases.

She checked the camera every few seconds to make sure she wasn't somehow recording the ceiling, or her own face. When she was satisfied the angle was right, Agnes took in the action.

Vivianne kept pulling articles out of her pocket and trying to break them in the moments her body responded. Lionel's binding spell was doing a good job of interrupting her but couldn't seem to hold her for more than a few moments.

She didn't understand why Rhodri and Lionel didn't simply grab her and tie her up like a human would. Leith climbed onto the counter and crouched. "Duck." He tossed a length of black cord toward them.

It floated over their heads and circled Vivianne, dropping to tighten around her body, pulling her arms to her side.

Finally.

Agnes looked at her screen again to make sure the camera focused on Vivianne. It did, and she watched in dismay as the cord twisted and started to fall apart.

The woman had too much power. It was only her against six full-sized people, but jammed in her corner, she was able to keep the attackers down to one or two.

Rhodri was mumbling words as he threw chalk toward Vivianne. She bent over in a coughing fit. Bramble took the opening and flew in to toss more chalk. He zipped back out of the way, joining Agnes in the corner.

"She will run out of spells at some point," Bramble said. "It is tiring, but we have the advantage."

He didn't look that confident. Agnes scanned the room. "Where is Fernlight?"

"She is waiting outside with Kim," Bramble said. "Mamoru is on his way. He will not be able to help. When we contain her, then he can arrest her. I think we should be able to do that."

A step too far for now.

"The brownies?" Agnes glanced at her screen again. The three men were continuing a barrage of spells and Vivianne, no longer coughing, countered each one.

"Who knows?" Bramble said. "Perhaps they went for reinforcements? It would be easier to trust them if they didn't just go off on their own."

A shout of pain brought Agnes's attention back to the fight. Leith was holding his arm, blood flowing through.

Bramble flew over and pulled him into the living room. "I'm too small to fix this," he said. "I will hold your phone and you can bandage him." He didn't wait for her response, just grabbed the phone and hovered near the ceiling.

Agnes bent to look at the wound. "What happened?"

"I am embarrassed to say that I forgot that mundane

things like knives exist. She threw one and I didn't dodge fast enough. You can tear my shirt to use as a bandage."

The noise in the kitchen quieted. Agnes wrapped Leith's arm and told him to apply pressure, that an ambulance would come soon.

"No need. If there are no healing charms here, I will survive until someone can make one."

She stood and looked at the kitchen. Leith's injury had not been in vain. Apparently, knives were not the only thing that could be used. Someone had wrapped Vivianne from chest to shins in a long rope.

"It will not hold long," Pit shouted. "Look, it is already fraying. You must think of something quickly."

"You can't win," Vivianne said, her voice hoarse. "There are too many of us."

"She is confessing!" Bramble shouted. He handed Agnes her phone and started to float toward the kitchen.

"Bramble, do not trust her," Leith called. "I do not wish to report your loss to my queen."

Bramble floated back to them. Agnes waited for the usual bickering.

"She cares about me?"

Leith chuckled. "She cares about our honor."

"Hurry," Pit called. "The rope is loosening."

Agnes turned her attention back to the fight. Lionel and Rhodri were both panting. If they didn't act soon, they would lose the advantage.

"You can't contain me," Vivianne said. "You may have been born to magic, but you don't improve it. Look how we used your simple spells to create weapons. Ones even you can't defeat."

Lionel tossed a small stone at her feet. "All magic items from this woman must answer the call," he announced.

Agnes had never heard him be so commanding. And then

she realized it was a spell. Seeds, nuts, ribbons, and dust drifted to the stone. They didn't crust the surface, they sank in.

The rope stopped fraying. Vivianne struggled in her bonds. "You haven't won. I am not alone in this."

"She is lying," Pit said. "Can't you hear it?"

"I have many people begging for the results of my work," she screamed. "They will make sure I am free."

Bramble buzzed to the woman. "You killed our friend. No one will be able to protect you from the magical revenge." He flew back to Agnes before Vivianne could react.

"Magical revenge?" Agnes asked. "That will need to be explained." She nodded to her phone, still recording.

Bramble flew in close to whisper, "There is no such thing. I wanted to worry her."

"Tell Fernlight and Kim they can come in," Rhodri said.

"Wait," Leith said, struggling to his feet. "In the excitement I forgot to check. Grant Norman is no longer in the hands of HOP-D."

CHAPTER SIXTY-ONE

The door swung open as Bramble turned to warn Fernlight and Kim. Too late. They were already caught. Behind them, holding a gun, stood Grant Norman, covered in blood. Bramble couldn't see any damage, so it was probably not his, but if HOP-D beat him up, Bramble didn't care.

"Let them go," he said, rushing to try to scratch the man's eyes.

Grant dodged and then looked at Vivianne. Bramble tried to swoop in again, but Fernlight gave him a stern look. Fairies could fly faster than bullets, but perhaps she worried about the people who couldn't. He flew backward, keeping his eyes firmly on Grant Norman's face.

"Looks like you need some help," Grant called into Vivianne. "Didn't your magic work?"

Everyone watched the gun. Bramble searched in his head for a spell to melt it, but there was nothing to find. And his power was getting weak again.

Grant used the gun to make everyone leave the kitchen. He stood with Vivianne. He reached and undid the knot holding the rope tight.

In a moment, Vivianne stepped out of the pile of rope on the floor. "They took my spells. What did you bring?"

"Nothing. Remember, I've been at HOP-D wasting their time."

He looked over her shoulder out the window to the neighbor's backyard.

Bramble followed his gaze. A little house peeked over the fence. The kind humans used as garden sheds. It sat far from the other house.

Where is Pit now that he can help?

Bramble called his name in the fairy register. He was happy when Vivianne winced and tapped her ear.

"What?" Pit stood on the mantle next to where Bramble floated.

"Did you check the little house?" He wanted to point, but it would tell everyone they were talking.

"It is not her house. The warrant—"

"Don't worry about that. If there is nothing inside, no one will know. If we find something important, we will figure out a way to make it legal."

"Rules are very confusing," Pit said. "And that woman hears us."

Bramble smiled right at Vivianne. "Not our words, but I have an idea. Can you leave some of your horde here and tell them to do what I say?"

Pit looked at him and Bramble knew right away the sneaky brownie was going to ruin everything.

"I will leave Shade and the horde. I can search alone."

He climbed down the wall like a spider, passing Shade as she came up.

"What is your idea?" Shade asked.

"Do brownies sing like fairies?" Bramble asked. Grant still pointed the gun at them, but Vivianne was reaching into the back of a cupboard.

"Why?"

Bramble stopped looking at the two humans to glare at Shade. "Why do you always ask questions?"

"I am a brownie. We are curious."

"Do you see her face when we talk?" He pointed to Vivianne, who was now putting a tin on the counter.

"She doesn't like it. That's odd. Kim and Agnes don't even notice."

"How do you think she would react to all of us singing?"

Shade giggled. "That is a very good idea. But what about the man?"

Bramble had no idea what to do about the gun. "Do you know a melting spell?"

"No. What are you going to do with our singing? That tin she pulled out has magic. It hid from us."

Bramble's plan was simple. The fairies and brownies were too small to fight the same way, but they could help the bigger people. And Agnes would just have to live with the magic.

"A molasses spell."

"Use it on the gun too," Shade said. "We will sing and hurt her ears, so she won't use those charms. You can use the molasses spell on both, and the big ones can tie them up and we will all be safe, and they will be arrested."

Bramble heard a car pull up. "Send someone to keep the new people outside," he said. "We don't need any more complications."

Shade nodded and looked down at the horde. Bramble didn't take his eyes off the criminals.

"Another portal spell," Shade said. "She will escape."

"Let's hope everyone figures it out," Bramble said.

"I hear your plan," Leith's voice said. "It is hard for me to talk at this range, but I am ready."

"What are you doing?" Grant asked Vivianne.

"I'll come back for you," she said. "Just keep them away."

"I'm not doing your bidding anymore," Grant said. He glared at Vivianne and didn't notice the gun in his hand wander to point at her.

"Now!" Bramble said.

The entire horde started singing a complicated song about a legend. Bramble flew to the kitchen and cast the molasses spell.

Leith pulled Lionel with him to the kitchen. "Hurry, we don't know if they can counter it."

Leith must have had a spell to counter the molasses because Lionel and Rhodri moved at their usual speed.

Vivianne cried and held her ears, so she couldn't use any of her charms.

Bramble looked out the window and saw two people coming across the backyard. One of them was Raj.

"You can let the police in now," he said to Shade. "You did a good job." He didn't even feel mad that they looked like the heroes.

CHAPTER SIXTY-TWO

Agnes turned off the camera. Her arm ached as though it had been hours, but the whole fight took less than ten minutes. Fernlight offered to ease the pain with magic, and Agnes was grateful.

The wound in Leith's arm needed far less attention than Agnes expected. The blood already staunched before Rhodri used a salve to start the flesh knitting together.

"No scar," he said. "I promise you will be as perfect as before."

"Thank you," Leith said.

The police placed their two criminals in handcuffs and waited for Mamoru to instruct them.

Raj was in the kitchen, holding a damp cloth to his swollen nose and giving his statement. The other man, the minister, said he would talk after he called his wife. He did not look beaten at all.

Agnes wanted to hear the stories in full and would happily wait until the investigators finished. Even if she was forced to travel through the magical paths. Then again, perhaps Mamoru would arrange a car for the human contingent.

"We will sort out the procedural issues later," Mamoru said. "You all look in need of rest. Shall we say ten o'clock in your office?"

"Can we get a ride?" Kim asked. "I do not have the strength to walk underground again."

"Do we know why this all happened?" Agnes asked as she picked up her bag. "It all seems a little James Bond villain."

She handed Mamoru her phone so he could send a copy of her video somewhere.

Mamoru rolled his eyes in an uncharacteristic show of emotion. "She says it's because the magical folk were preparing to take over the world. She was saving us all. For our own good."

"That rationale sounds familiar," Agnes said. "So much evil done for our own good."

He nodded, neither of them needing to acknowledge the details of their history with evil done in the name of good intentions.

CHAPTER SIXTY-THREE

Bramble landed on the desk, calling his children to join him. It was after ten o'clock and time to hear what HOP-D had found out. The humans still looked a little tired, but they were alert. Even Agnes had come, but this time she didn't look like she would be taking notes.

Mamoru leaned against the wall. "We were able to get most of the story," he said. "It is amazing how people turn on each other when they think it will ease their punishment."

"Please just tell us," Bramble said. "I know we don't have any cases to work on, but I am going to explode if you don't tell us."

Mamoru nodded. "There will be other cases and soon, I'm sure. For the future, you will need to learn how to give evidence. Neither of these two will confess, so we are going to court. Agnes agreed to help you with that."

So that's why she is here. Now she isn't going to try to stop us doing magic, I can like her all the time.

"It will fit in with her original mandate, which is not finished," Mamoru said as if he'd read Bramble's mind.

"Well?" Raj asked. He was still covered in bruises. "What did you learn?"

Mamoru folded his arms across his chest and started speaking.

"Vivianne Braithwaite is the brain behind *Sla Styrkur*. About two months after the prophecy that revealed your world to us, she created the company and has been building on her plans ever since. Let's do this in order, as far as we know it."

Yes, hurry!

"When she saw the possibilities of Heath's work, she tried to convince him to join her. Apparently, she couldn't believe the usual appeal of money or power didn't work on him. She ordered Brigit to kill him because she figured she'd find another wizard to fill his place."

"Did she?" Bramble asked. "I hope not. But Lionel has all of Heath's things now and maybe someone like her will kill him."

Lionel shook his head. "Bramble, I will be fine."

"She did not," Mamoru said. "It still amazes her that wizards can't be bought."

"And we are on alert for people like her now," Lionel said.

"She also said Heath was working with other companies. If we find any proof of that, we will do a check on their ambitions."

Bramble remembered the garden company from the last case. *Maybe they will all be like that. Kind, not mean and greedy.*

"They took Raj because he did a search on the companies at HOP-D. I would be interested in how you manage to hide your own research efforts. That is a useful tool, and no one will have any legitimate questions about it."

"I didn't realize we were hiding anything," Lionel said. "We will look into it. Please, continue with your story."

"We caught her just in time," Mamoru said. "She had no

customers, and she had not yet put out feelers for them. The minister was taken because he worked closely with Maeve. Prior ministers in the portfolio did not seem interested in making progress. Vivianne feared her efforts would be uncovered if a curious human got involved."

"And the dead body, the one with the charm inside?" Bramble asked.

"An experiment," Mamoru said. "She was attempting to use the charm to control a subject. It did not work, but I am sure she hadn't finished with the idea."

"That's it?" Bramble asked. "She was only greedy and mean?"

"And Grant became a useful tool," Mamoru said. "As far as we know, this closes all the cases on the books. But as I said, there will be others. Vivianne is not unique. And crimes where magic is involved don't necessarily come with such grand plans. You might enjoy a more ordinary case or two."

"Don't worry," Kim said. "We'll be writing reports and answering questions for a while. Not having a case doesn't mean we'll be sitting around drinking martinis."

"And one other thing," Mamoru said. "I reviewed the video of your fight with Vivianne."

"We had to do magic! She was doing magic!" Bramble hadn't meant to shout, but he was very tired of having to prove magic was good.

"Yes. And the magic you used will be helpful to other investigations. I think we need to talk about how HOP-D human investigators might use things like your spell to slow someone down."

Someone else can do that. I will not work with any more humans than these three right now. Bramble didn't say anything. Fernlight could decide how to tell Mamoru no.

WANT MORE?

Looking for more great reads? Use the QR code to check out the books on pawilson.ca

If you enjoyed reading Deadly Magic Dance, please consider helping other readers to find the story by leaving a review.

FREE EBOOK

Claim your copy of Spells and Other Charms when you use the QR code to sign up for my newsletter and learn more about Quinn and Cate's past.

ALSO BY P A WILSON

For more books by P A Wilson

Use the QR code below or go to pawilson.ca

ABOUT THE AUTHOR

Perry Wilson is a Canadian author based in Vancouver, BC who has big ideas and an itch to tell stories. Having spent some time on university, a career, and life in general, she returned to writing in 2008 and hasn't looked back since (well, maybe a little, but only while parallel parking).

She is a member of the Vancouver Writers Social Group, The Royal City Literary Arts Society, and The Surrey Writing Workshop. Perry has self-published several novels. She writes the Madeline Journeys, a fantasy series about a high-powered lawyer who finds herself trapped in a magical world, the Quinn Larson Quests, which follows the adventures of a wizard named Quinn who must contend with volatile fae in the heart of Vancouver, and the Charity Deacon Investigations, a mystery thriller series about a private eye who tends to fall into serious trouble with her cases, and The Riverton Romances, a series based in a small town in Oregon, one of her favorite states. Her stand-alone novels are Breaking the Bonds, Closing the Circle, and The Dragon at The Edge of The Map.

For more information
www.pawilson.ca
pawilson@pawilson.ca

ACKNOWLEDGMENTS

People think that the process of writing is solitary. That's not the case for me. I have help from so many people it would be hard to acknowledge everyone, but I'll give it a try.

The support and inspiration I get from my writer's groups is incalculable. The Vancouver Writers Social Group opens my mind to other ways of telling a story. The Royal City Literary Arts Society gives me the opportunity to meet and share with other writers who have more knowledge than I do. The Other 11 Months group is where I learn about getting the words on the page. And my critique group who helps me find the best parts of the story I want to tell. Thanks to all of the members of these great groups.

Last of all, but definitely a huge part of the process, my beta readers. These are the people who love stories and are willing, and more than able, to tell me if my finished story is ready for you, my readers.